JEDI APPRENTICE

The Defenders of the Dead

Jude Watson

SCHOLASTIC INC.

New York Toronto London Auckland Sydney
Mexico City New Delhi Hong Kong

No part of this publication may be reproduced in whole or in part, or stored in a retrieval system or transmitted in any form or by any means, electronic, mechanical, photocopying, recording, or otherwise, without written permission of the publisher. For information regarding permission, write to Scholastic Inc., Attention: Permissions Department, 555 Broadway, New York, NY 10012.

ISBN 0-590-51956-5

12 11 10 9 8 7 6 5 4 3 2 1   9/9 0 1/2 3 4/0

Printed in the U.S.A.
First Scholastic printing, December 1999

CHAPTER 1

The starfighter darted closer to the surface of the planet Melida/Daan. On the rugged terrain below, vast structures made of ebony stone hugged the ground, laid out in enormous perfect squares without windows or doors.

Obi-Wan Kenobi studied them through the viewscreen as he piloted the craft. "What do you think they are?" he asked Qui-Gon Jinn. "I've never seen anything like them."

"I don't know," the Jedi Knight replied, studying the landscape with keen blue eyes. "Storage warehouses, perhaps, or military installations."

"They could conceal tracking devices," Obi-Wan observed.

"I'm not picking up anything on the scanner. But let's fly lower just in case."

Without slowing, Obi-Wan piloted the craft closer to the planet's surface. Rocks and vegetation rushed past the viewscreen. With the engines at full power Obi-Wan kept a tight grip on the controls. One tiny adjustment could send them crashing.

"If we fly any lower, I'll be able to do a molecular scan of the topsoil," Qui-Gon remarked dryly from the copilot's seat. "You're flying too low at this speed, Padawan. If we come across a stray boulder, we may end up making an unscheduled crash landing."

His tone was mild, but Obi-Wan knew Qui-Gon would accept no argument. Obi-Wan was Qui-Gon's Jedi apprentice, and one of the Jedi rules was not to question the order of a Master.

Reluctantly, Obi-Wan eased up slightly on the controls. The starfighter rose a few meters. Qui-Gon stared steadily ahead, still searching for a place to land. They were reaching the outskirts of Zehava, the main city on the planet of Melida/Daan, and it was crucial that their arrival be unnoticed.

The bloody civil war on Melida/Daan had been raging for thirty years. It was a continuation of a conflict that had lasted for centuries. The two warring peoples, the Melida and the Daan, couldn't even agree on a name for their planet. The Melida called it Melida and the Daan called it Daan. In a compromise, the Galactic Senate used both names separated by a slash mark.

Every town and city on the planet was hotly contested, with territory taken and lost in a continuing series of battles. The capital city of Zehava was under siege much of the time, as the boundaries between Daan and Melida constantly shifted.

Obi-Wan knew that Jedi Master Yoda was depending on them for success in this mission. He had chosen carefully among the many Jedi. This mission was important to him. Weeks ago, one of his brightest pupils, the Jedi Knight Tahl, had come to Melida/Daan as a guardian of peace.

Tahl was renowned among the Jedi Knights for her diplomatic skills. The two sides had been close to a settlement when war broke out again. Tahl had been badly wounded and captured by the Melida.

Just days ago, Yoda had succeeded in getting a message through to his original contact, a Melida named Wehutti. Wehutti had agreed to smuggle Obi-Wan and Qui-Gon into the city and help them to work for Tahl's release.

The mission ahead was more difficult and dangerous than usual, Obi-Wan knew. This time, the Jedi had not been invited to settle a dispute. They were unwelcome. The last Jedi envoy had been captured, perhaps killed.

He glanced over at his Master. Qui-Gon's calm,

steady gaze swept the landscape ahead. He betrayed no agitation or worry that Obi-Wan could see.

One of the many things Obi-Wan admired about Master Qui-Gon was his composure. He had wanted to become Qui-Gon's Padawan because Qui-Gon was well respected for his bravery, skill, and ability with the Force. Although they sometimes had their differences, Obi-Wan had a deep respect for the Jedi Master.

"Do you see that canyon?" Qui-Gon asked, leaning forward and pointing. "If you can land between the walls, we can hide the starfighter there. It's a tight fit."

"I can do it," Obi-Wan promised. Keeping his speed steady, he dipped down lower.

"Slow down," Qui-Gon warned.

"I can make it," Obi-Wan said, gritting his teeth. He was one of the better pilots at the Jedi Temple. Why did Qui-Gon always have to correct him?

He zoomed into the small clearing with only a centimeter to spare. But at the last moment — too late — he saw that one of the cliffs had a small outcropping. A groaning sound filled the cockpit as the side of the ship scraped against it.

Obi-Wan set the craft down and powered down the engines. He did not want to look at

Qui-Gon. But he knew that being a Jedi meant taking responsibility for every mistake. He met his Master's gaze squarely.

He was relieved to see amusement in Qui-Gon's eyes. "At least we didn't promise to return the starfighter without a scratch," he said.

Obi-Wan grinned. They had borrowed the transport from Queen Veda on the planet Gala, where they had successfully completed their last mission.

As they climbed down from the starfighter onto the rocky terrain of Melida/Daan, Qui-Gon paused. "There is a great disturbance in the Force on this world," he murmured. "Hatred rules this place."

"Yes, I feel it," Obi-Wan said.

"We must be very careful here, Padawan. When so much volatile emotion is packed into a place, it is hard to keep your distance. Remember you are a Jedi. You are here to observe and to help where you can. Our mission is to return Tahl to the Temple."

"Yes, Master."

The underbrush was thick and leafy, and it was easy to drag large branches and cover the starfighter. It would not be visible from the air.

Shouldering their survival packs, the two Jedi headed toward the outskirts of Zehava. They had been instructed to approach from the west, where Wehutti would meet them at a Melida-controlled gate.

It was a dusty hike through hills and canyons. At last the towers and buildings of the walled city were before them. They had kept off the main road, keeping to open country, and now they looked down at the city from a nearby cliff.

Keeping low to the ground, Obi-Wan scanned the desolate outskirts of the city. He saw no people on the streets. There was only one entrance to the city on the main road. At the break in the thick wall a guardhouse stood, bristling with laser cannons trained on the road. Two tall deflection towers flanked the guardhouse. Behind the wall they could glimpse the buildings perched on the steep hills of the city. Close to the wall was a long, low building of black stone, with no windows or doors.

"It's a smaller version of those square buildings we saw from the air," Obi-Wan observed.

Qui-Gon nodded. "It could be a military building of some kind. And those deflection towers mean that there is a particle shield in place. If we attempt to enter without permission, we'll be blasted with laser fire."

"What should we do?" Obi-Wan asked. "We don't want to approach unless we're sure Wehutti is there."

Qui-Gon dug in his survival pack for a pair of electrobinoculars. He trained them on the guardhouse. "I've got worse news," he said. "I see a Daan flag. That means either the whole city is now controlled by the Daan, or the entrance is."

"And Wehutti is a Melida." Obi-Wan groaned. "So there's no way in."

Qui-Gon scuttled back to remove himself from sight. He slid the electrobinoculars back into his pack. "There is always a way, Padawan," he said. "Wehutti told us to approach from the west. If we follow the perimeter, we might find an unguarded area. Perhaps he's on the lookout. Once we're away from that guard tower, we can get closer."

Keeping to the cover of the shadow of the cliffs, Obi-Wan and Qui-Gon made their painstaking way around the city's walls. When they were out of the guardhouse's sight, they moved closer. Qui-Gon's keen eyes swept every meter of the wall, searching for a break. Obi-Wan knew he was using the Force to test the way ahead, hoping to sense a break in the particle shield. Obi-Wan tried to do the same, but he could only feel glimmers of resistance.

"Wait," Qui-Gon said suddenly. He stopped and held up a hand. "Here. There's a break in the shield."

"There's another one of those black buildings,"

Obi-Wan pointed out. The long, low building sat next to the wall on the city side.

"I still don't know what they are, but I suggest we avoid them," Qui-Gon remarked. "We'll scale the wall near those trees."

"We'll need the Force," Obi-Wan said, eyeing the high wall.

"Yes, but a carbon rope would help, too," Qui-Gon said, smiling. He put his pack down, then leaned over to root through it. "We'll need yours, too, Padawan."

Obi-Wan stepped closer to Qui-Gon, swinging his pack off his shoulder to the ground. His boots suddenly hit something with a clang. He looked down and saw he had displaced some dirt on top of a metal plate. "Look, Master," he said. "I wonder what this —"

He didn't get a chance to finish. Energy bars suddenly rose from the ground, trapping them. Before they could move, the metal plate slid open, and they fell into an abyss below.

CHAPTER 2

Obi-Wan was falling through some sort of metal tube. He tried to slow his descent with his heels, but they only clattered against the rough metal surface. His speed increased, and he tumbled forward, hitting his head on the edge of the tube and then spilling out onto a dirt floor.

He lay for a moment, stunned. Qui-Gon picked himself up immediately, his lightsaber in hand. He stood over Obi-Wan in case he needed protection.

"I'm all right," Obi-Wan said, his head clearing. He struggled to his feet, grabbing his lightsaber as he did so. "Where are we?"

"In some sort of holding cell," Qui-Gon answered. Smooth durasteel walls surrounded them. There was no crack or opening that Obi-Wan could see.

"We're trapped," he said. His voice bounced off the walls, sounding hollow.

"No, Padawan," Qui-Gon said quietly. "There is more than one entrance to this cell."

"How do you know?"

"Because we are not the first to fall into it." Qui-Gon explored the tiny space, using his lightsaber for illumination. "The tube we fell down is battered, and the dirt is disturbed by other footprints. The others have been taken out somehow, and it would be impossible to do so from the way we came in. This trap is engineered to capture, not kill. There must be another door. Besides," he added, "there are no bones or remains. That means that whoever set the trap removes who they capture."

"Eventually," Obi-Wan muttered. His stomach was empty, and he wished he'd had time to eat before he'd left the starfighter. "I lost my survival pack," he told Qui-Gon. "It's on the surface."

"Mine is as well. We'll have to use our lightsabers," Qui-Gon replied.

Obi-Wan had food in mind more than illumination, but he followed Qui-Gon's example and activated his lightsaber. He held it close to the walls surrounding him, examining them. As he worked, he felt the Force begin to move between them, filling the space.

He clearly saw every irregularity in the seemingly smooth walls. He searched for a hidden seam, sure now that they would find one. All he had to do was trust the Force.

As a student at the Temple, he had been mystified by the Force. He knew he was Force-sensitive — it was why he had been chosen to study at the Temple as a child. But throughout his training, he often found the Force elusive and unreliable. He was able to tap into it, but not every time he wanted to. When he did, he could not control it.

With Qui-Gon, he had learned that it was not his job to control it, but to join it. Now he could rely on it to guide him, give him strength and vision. He was beginning to understand how deeply it pulsed, how steady a presence it was. As a Jedi, he had constant access to it. It was the greatest gift he could imagine being given.

"Here," Qui-Gon said quietly.

At first, Obi-Wan could not see anything. But then he noticed the tiny hairline crack in the even surface of the wall.

Qui-Gon moved his hand over the seam. "Of course the locking device is on the other side," he mused. "I'm assuming it's blast-proof. But I'm also assuming that no Jedi has ever been trapped here before."

Together, Obi-Wan and Qui-Gon moved the beams of their lightsabers down the outline of the door. The sabers cut through the metal, which curled back like a tender green leaf. A small opening was exposed.

Qui-Gon squeezed through, and Obi-Wan followed. He found himself in a short, narrow tunnel, which led to what he sensed was a huge space. It was pitch-dark, a darkness so black it held no shadows. Even the glow of his lightsaber seemed swallowed up by the absolute darkness.

They stopped, listening carefully. But not a sound moved through the space. Obi-Wan could not even hear his breathing, or Qui-Gon's. Jedi are trained to slow their breath so they make no sound, even when they are under pressure or stress.

"I think we are alone," Qui-Gon said quietly. His voice echoed, confirming Obi-Wan's belief that they were in a wide, open space.

They moved forward cautiously, lightsabers held in defensive position. Obi-Wan felt a trickle of perspiration snake down the back of his neck. Something was wrong here. He could feel it.

"The Force is dark," Qui-Gon murmured. "Angry. Yet I don't feel a living Force here."

Obi-Wan nodded. He could not have put his finger on what he felt, but Qui-Gon had been able to. Some deep-rooted evil was here, yet he did not feel a living pulse around him.

Obi-Wan's foot hit a ledge that he hadn't been

able to see. He reached out to steady himself against a stone column. In that split-second of lost concentration, a flicker of movement came from his right.

He whirled, lightsaber held high. A warrior appeared, moving quickly toward him from the deep shadows, his blaster aimed straight at Obi-Wan's heart.

CHAPTER 3

Obi-Wan sprang, his lightsaber slashing forward. The beam did not meet flesh or bone, but passed harmlessly through the figure.

Surprised, Obi-Wan whirled to the left to launch another attack, but Qui-Gon stopped him.

"You cannot fight this enemy, Padawan," Qui-Gon said.

Obi-Wan looked closer. The warrior, he realized, was a hologram.

Suddenly, a voice boomed out. "I am Quintama, Captain of the Melida Liberation Force." The hologram moved his blaster to his side. "Tomorrow will commence the Twenty-First Battle of Zehava. It will doom our Daan enemies to destruction once and for all, and we shall achieve glorious victory. We shall recapture the city that we founded a thousand years ago. All Melida will live in peace."

"Twenty-First Battle of Zehava?" Obi-Wan whispered to Qui-Gon.

"The city has changed hands many times over the years," Qui-Gon remarked. "Look at his blaster. It's an old model. I'd say fifty years or more."

"I look forward to glorious total victory," the ghostly figure continued. "And yet there is a chance that in achieving that victory I will die. I accept my death willingly, as does my wife Pinani, who fights by my side. But for my children . . ." The booming voice faltered for only a moment. ". . . My children, Renei and Wunana, I leave the memory of the ancestors I have shared with them, the stories of our long persecution by the Daan. I saw my father killed, and I will avenge his death. I saw my village starved, and I will avenge my neighbors. Remember me, my children. And remember what I have suffered at the hands of the Daan. If I die, pick up my weapon and avenge me as I have avenged my family." Abruptly, the hologram disappeared.

"I guess he didn't make it," Obi-Wan said. He crouched down to a stone marker. "He died in that battle."

Qui-Gon moved past the marker and came to the next. A large golden ball was mounted on a column next to it. He placed his hand on it.

Immediately, another hologram rose from its marker like a ghost.

"I must have triggered the first one when I stumbled," Obi-Wan said.

The second hologram was a woman. Her tunic was torn and stained, her hair clipped short. She carried a force pike and had one blaster strapped to a hip, another to a thigh.

"I am Pinani, widow of Quintama, daughter of the great heroes Bicha and Tiraca. Tonight we march on the town of Bin to avenge the Battle of Zehava. Our supplies have been depleted. Our weapons are low. Most of us died in the glorious battle to retake our beloved city of Zehava from the ruthless Daan. There is no chance that our battle will succeed, yet we will fight for justice and vengeance against the enemy who persecutes us. My husband died before my eyes. My father and mother died when the Daan marched into our village and rounded them up and killed them. And so I say to you, my children, Renei and Wunana, do not forget us. Fight on. Avenge this great terrible wrong. I will die bravely. I die for you."

The hologram blinked out. Obi-Wan crossed to the next marker. "Renei and Wunana both died only three years later in the Twenty-Second Battle of Zehava," he said. "They were barely older than me."

He turned and met Qui-Gon's eyes. "What kind of place is this?" he asked.

"A mausoleum," Qui-Gon said. "A place for the dead to rest. But here on Melida/Daan, the memories stay alive. Look." Qui-Gon pointed to the offerings that they now saw heaped on pedestals in front of the columns. The flowers were fresh, the trays of seeds and cups of water replenished.

They walked down the aisles, past row after row of graves, activating hologram after hologram. The vast, echoing space filled with the voices of the dead. They saw generations tell their stories of blood and vengeance. They heard tales of whole villages starved and then slaughtered, children torn from their mother's arms, mass executions, forced marches that ended in suffering and more death.

"The Daan sound like a bloodthirsty people," Obi-Wan remarked. The accounts of suffering and agony had moved through him like growing pain from a deep wound.

"We're in a Melida mausoleum," Qui-Gon replied. "I wonder what the Daan have to say."

"There are so many dead," Obi-Wan observed. "But there's no clear reason why they fight. Battle follows battle, each one conducted to avenge the one before. What is the real dispute?"

"Perhaps they have forgotten it," Qui-Gon said. "The hatred is bred in their bones. Now they fight over meters of territory, or to avenge a wrong that happened a hundred years before."

Obi-Wan shivered. The damp, cold air had invaded his body. He felt cut away from the rest of the galaxy. His world had funneled down into this black, shadowy space full of blood, revenge, and death. "Our mission here hasn't even begun, and already I have seen enough suffering to last a lifetime."

Qui-Gon's gaze was sad. "There are some worlds that manage to hold onto peace for centuries, Padawan. But I am afraid that many have seen terrible wars that scar the memories of each generation. It has always been."

"Well, I've seen enough for now," Obi-Wan said. "Let's find the way out."

They walked quickly now, hurrying past the markers, searching for an exit. At last they saw a square of brightness ahead. It was a door fashioned from a translucent material that emitted a white glow.

Qui-Gon pressed the exit indicator light, and they spilled out into the weak sunshine with relief. They remained in the shadow of the doorway, scanning the immediate area before moving on.

The mausoleum was perched on a ridge. Ahead of them rose a steep hill that ended in an overhanging cliff. A path wound through gardens to their left, a wall to their right.

"I guess we have to go that way," Obi-Wan said, pointing to the path.

"I suppose," Qui-Gon said. Still, he hesitated, his keen gaze searching the steep hillside in front of them. "But I —"

Suddenly, the dirt exploded in front of Obi-Wan's feet.

"Snipers!" Qui-Gon yelled. "Take cover!"

CHAPTER 4

The blaster fire came from the top of the overhanging cliff. Obi-Wan and Qui-Gon leaped to the top of the wall on their right. Chips of stone splintered and flew as blaster fire ripped into the wall. Qui-Gon took a split-second to balance and survey what lay below. Then he leaped down, Obi-Wan directly behind him.

They landed in a small area with humming banks of machinery. Walls surrounded them on three sides, the mausoleum building on the other. They would be trapped here under fire, but at least the blaster fire could not reach them. Qui-Gon wondered fleetingly if the snipers would get bored and go away.

Unfortunately, in his long experience, snipers *never* got bored and went away.

Qui-Gon examined the machinery. "These must be the heating and cooling units for the building," he observed as blaster fire continued to rip over their heads.

"At least we're out of the line of fire," Obi-Wan said.

"I'm afraid we have a bigger problem," Qui-Gon said. He bent down to examine a metal tank. "This is full of proton fuel. If the blaster fire hits it, we'll be blown from here back to the starship."

He exchanged a concerned glance with Obi-Wan. They would have to expose themselves to the snipers. They could not remain here and continue to draw fire.

"Let's see what's on the other side of that wall," Qui-Gon said, indicating the wall opposite to the one they had leaped over.

Obi-Wan and Qui-Gon summoned the Force. When Qui-Gon felt it grow and pulse around them, he jumped, along with Obi-Wan. As they leaped into midair, they took a quick survey of what lay on the other side, blaster fire suddenly intensifying around them. Qui-Gon deflected it with his lightsaber.

They fell back to the ground.

"It's a big drop down to that ravine," Obi-Wan reported to Qui-Gon. "Do you think we can make it?"

"The ground looks soft," Qui-Gon said. "That could help our landing, but if it's swampy, we could be in trouble. We don't want to be swallowed by a bog. Remember that the terrain of Melida/Daan can be treacherous."

"At least we'll surprise the snipers," Obi-Wan pointed out. "They won't expect us to risk it."

Qui-Gon nodded. "We can work our way around the cliff and scale it from the other side to surprise them further. The brush will cover us. They won't know which way we went, and probably won't expect us to attack."

"The only alternative, Master, is to go back over the wall. Once we made it to that path, we'd have shelter in the gardens."

Qui-Gon paused, thinking of their next move. While he considered the odds, he thought about the way he and Obi-Wan had come to function together as a unit. Though at times their relations could be bumpy, under pressure their rhythm matched, their thoughts clicked. He admired his Padawan's ability to operate on all levels. Even under great pressure, Obi-Wan could strategize, calculate odds and opportunities, and make a joke.

"If we try for the gardens, we lose the element of surprise," Qui-Gon said finally. "Remember this, Padawan: when one is outnumbered, surprise is your best ally. Let's try the ravine."

Blaster fire pinged against metal, and Qui-

Gon flicked an apprehensive gaze at the proton gas tank. "I think it's time we left. Don't forget there's a line of shrubs at the immediate bottom of the slope on the other side. Make your jump as wide as you can."

Qui-Gon reached out for the Force. It was always there, ready for him to tap into. It was his companion as much as Obi-Wan was. He pictured the leap he would have to make. Nothing was impossible when the Force was near. His body would do what it needed to do.

They backed up as far as they could for a running start. Then they ran forward three quick steps and took the leap. They cleared the wall easily — the Force and the momentum sent them sailing through the air, over the steep slope into the ravine.

Qui-Gon felt the swampy ground move under his feet as he landed, but it did not suck him down. Obi-Wan landed softly a short distance behind him.

"Hurry, Padawan," Qui-Gon urged.

Mud sucked at their boots, hampering their progress as they struggled to make their way around the cliff face. They could hear the blaster fire and then the thump of a proton grenade exploding. Qui-Gon turned. The grenade had fallen just short of the walled enclosure. But if one scored a direct hit on the proton fuel tank, it could help them. An explosion would be good cover for a successful assault.

At last they made it to the opposite side of the cliff. Here, the rocky ground sloped sharply upward. It would be a steep climb, but at least the ground was firm.

Obi-Wan moved quickly and tirelessly beside him, his physical strength backed by his strong will. Obi-Wan would learn grace as he grew older, Qui-Gon knew.

They slowed their ascent as they grew closer to the top of the hill. Surprise was not only helpful, but necessary. They had no idea how many snipers they would find.

When they were close to the top, Qui-Gon gave the signal and they dropped to their knees. They lay flat, then squirmed up the remaining distance on their stomachs. Qui-Gon guided them to the shelter of a cluster of boulders at the hill's edge.

Four snipers were lined up on the cliff face, laying flat with their blasters pointed toward the mausoleum. Not bad odds for a Jedi, Qui-Gon thought.

Silently, he drew his lightsaber. Obi-Wan did the same. At Qui-Gon's nod, the two of them leaped up, activating their lightsabers at the same time. They made barely a whisper of sound as they moved.

Qui-Gon headed for the largest, strongest-looking sniper. Obi-Wan leaped toward the sniper about to fire a blaster rifle. With a single blow of Obi-Wan's lightsaber, the blaster rifle cracked in two.

Qui-Gon struck down at the largest sniper's weapon, and the blaster flew from his hand. The sniper rolled away to avoid the next blow, kicking out at Qui-Gon as he did so. The blow connected, sending fire through Qui-Gon's ribcage and surprising him. He was also surprised to note the sniper had only one arm.

A third sniper moved toward Qui-Gon with a vibro-shiv. Qui-Gon turned quickly to his left to avoid the blade, slashing down with his lightsaber to disarm the sniper. Obi-Wan launched himself at the fourth sniper and kicked his blaster rifle off the cliff.

Qui-Gon somersaulted backward as the one-armed sniper fired from a blaster he'd retrieved from an ankle holster. The blaster fire just missed him. The second sniper, who had lost his vibro-shiv, threw a proton grenade at Qui-Gon. The Jedi Knight leaped out of the way, and it sailed over the cliff.

Qui-Gon whirled to disarm his one-armed opponent, but suddenly he was shaken by an enormous explosion. The grenade had hit the proton gas tank. Qui-Gon felt air move against his skin like a wall of fire. His Jedi reflexes helped him stand his ground. Obi-Wan was also prepared. But the fourth sniper lost his balance with a cry, tumbling over the edge of the cliff. He grabbed a root and hoisted himself uneasily back to safety. Obi-Wan hovered over him, lightsaber ready, prepared to defend himself if necessary.

Qui-Gon's one-armed adversary kept his blaster steady. He was a little older than Qui-Gon. Underneath his plastoid armor his body was lean and strong. Synth-flesh covered one cheek. Qui-Gon guessed it had been recently applied since it did not have a chance to knit into living flesh.

The one-armed man's eyes flicked to Qui-Gon's weapon, and he laughed. "Is that the famous lightsaber I've heard so much about?"

Surprised to find himself having a conversation with a man desperately trying to kill him, Qui-Gon nodded.

The man grinned. "Jedi! We thought you were Daan!"

Qui-Gon did not lower his lightsaber.

The man tossed his blaster aside. "Relax, Jedi. By the strength of our mothers and the valor of our fathers, this is no trick. I am your contact, Wehutti. So you're here after all!"

CHAPTER 5

"We were told to meet you on the outskirts of Zehava," Qui-Gon remarked as he deactivated his lightsaber.

"I apologize for failing to meet you," Wehutti said, striding forward to greet them. "The message I received from the Temple was garbled. The despicable and evil Daan often jam communications. I sent back a message I would meet with Jedi representatives, hoping I would get further instructions. Right now, we are in the sector that the Daan plundered from us in the Twenty-Second battle. Until we have our vengeance, they control the outskirts of the city. I've been sneaking over for three days now, hoping I would find you somehow." He extended his palm outward in the local greeting. "You must be Qui-Gon Jinn."

"This is my apprentice, Obi-Wan Kenobi," Qui-Gon said.

Obi-Wan bowed to Wehutti. He was grateful that they had found their contact. They had barely been on Melida/Daan for an hour, and it was already apparent what a treacherous place it was.

Wehutti introduced his comrades as Moahdi, Kejas, and Herut. Herut clutched his sore wrist and glowered at Obi-Wan, who tried to look friendly.

"It appears we are lucky to have found you," Qui-Gon said. "If the Daan control the perimeter, I'm surprised you would venture so far."

Wehutti's friendly face grew stony. "In the valiant spirit of our honored ancestors, we must protect our Hall of Evidence."

"Hall of Evidence?" Obi-Wan asked.

Wehutti gestured at the black monolith below where Qui-Gon and Obi-Wan had wandered. "It is where we store the honored memories of our glorious dead. They are all warriors and heroes. If the lowlife Daan had their way, they would destroy our most sacred places. We need to show them they cannot enter."

"So the Melida and the Daan are still at war," Qui-Gon said.

"No, we have a cease-fire at the moment," Wehutti said. He drew a circle in the dirt with the toe of his boot, then a larger circle around it.

"The bloodthirsty Daan drove the Melida from their homes and contained them here, in the Inner Hub." He pointed to the inner circle. "The barbarians surround us on the Outer Circle. But victory will come one day. We shall retake Zehava. Block by block we will move outward."

Qui-Gon eyed the blaster on the ground. "You have a cease-fire, but I see you still shoot."

"The day I put down my weapon is the day that the Melida are free," Wehutti said quietly.

"What about Jedi Knight Tahl?" Qui-Gon asked. "Do you have news?"

Wehutti nodded. "I have spoken to the Melida leaders. They have come to see that holding a Jedi will not help our cause. A bit more negotiation might be called for, but I have every certainty that she will be released to your care."

"That is good news," Qui-Gon said.

Wehutti nodded. "Now we must go. It isn't safe here. Like our martyred ancestors, we are in danger every moment." He turned to Moahdi, Kejas, and Herut. "Gather the weapons. See if you can find the blaster rifle below. I'll see you back in the Hub."

His three companions hurried off, gathering up the vibro-shiv and a damaged blaster before they left. Wehutti picked up his blaster and returned it to its holster. "We are very low on weapons," he explained to the Jedi. "Even damaged ones must be salvaged for the day of our vengeance."

"Are you low on med supplies as well?" Qui-Gon asked.

Wehutti nodded and pointed to his absent arm. "No plastoid limbs available, I'm afraid. Some were lucky to get them, but many were not. We ran through everything we had after the last battle of Zehava, and the government has no money to order more. But I do all right. The sacrifice of my people means more than my pain."

Qui-Gon touched the spot where Wehutti had hit him and winced. "You do just fine," he told his former attacker.

Wehutti led them back down the rocky slope and turned down a path that ran behind houses at the edge of a park. The park was filled with damaged and rusting starfighters and floaters.

"The Daan don't seem to have funds, either," Qui-Gon noted.

"The last war bankrupted both sides," Wehutti said cheerfully. "At least we're even." He handed the Jedi two yellow discs. "In case we're stopped, these are forged Daan identity cards. But let's hope we're not stopped."

Wehutti led them down twisting alleyways and through the rear gardens of grand houses, down tiny streets and over rooftops. If they saw people ahead, they ducked into the shadows of buildings, or simply turned in the opposite direction. A fine rain began to fall, keeping most people off the streets.

"You know the city well," Qui-Gon observed.

Wehutti's mouth twisted. "I lived in this area as a young man. Now I am forbidden to come here."

At last they reached a desolate area. The buildings were bombed out, the windows shattered.

"This used to be a Melida neighborhood," Wehutti explained. "Now the Daan control it, but no one will live here. Too close to Melida territory."

They hurried down the street. Ahead was a tall fence with two deflection towers flanking it. Cannons were trained at the street ahead.

"Don't worry," Wehutti said. "The guards know me."

They walked past the checkpoint with Wehutti giving a casual wave to the guards. They saluted him respectfully. Obi-Wan noted that they were older, possibly in their sixties. They seemed old to be guards.

Once in Melida territory, Obi-Wan tried to relax, but his nerves were still jumping. He felt just as apprehensive as he had in Daan territory. Maybe it was the severe disturbances he could feel in the Force. Qui-Gon strode by his side, his face impassive, but Obi-Wan knew his Master was alert and watchful.

Barricades and checkpoints were set up at almost every block. He could see the evidence of battles fought here: blaster and grenade blasts pockmarked the buildings, and many were in ruins. Everyone he saw on the streets carried weapons in plain view. It was like the planets he'd heard about in the far reaches of the galaxy, where no laws were followed.

"We noticed other Halls of Evidence as we flew over Melida/Daan," Qui-Gon remarked to Wehutti.

"We call our world Melida," Wehutti corrected Qui-Gon in a friendly way. "We do not link our great tradition to that of the filthy Daan. Yes, even the Daan have Halls of Evidence. Evidence of their lies, we say. We Melida visit our ancestors every week to hear their stories. We bring our children so we keep alive the history of injustices the Melida have suffered at the hands of the Daan. Nobody forgets. Nobody will ever forget."

Obi-Wan felt a chill at Wehutti's grim words. Even if the Daan were as bad as he said, how could they continue to wage battle after battle when they were destroying their world piece by piece? He could see that Zehava had once been a beautiful city. Now it was a ruin. By building these enormous Halls of Evidence, were they keeping history alive, or destroying their civilization?

And there was something else that was wrong here, Obi-Wan thought. Something that hovered at the back of his mind, something he couldn't quite place.

Obi-Wan's gaze moved absently down the street to a group of Melidas sitting outside at a café. The window of the restaurant had been blown out, and a fire had destroyed the interior, but the owner had set out tables and chairs on the walkway outside. A few tubs of blooming plants with bright red flowers struggled to add a cheerful note next to the bomb-blasted building.

Suddenly, Obi-Wan realized what was wrong. He hadn't seen anyone on the streets older than twenty or younger than fifty or so. Mostly, the streets were crowded with elders and young people like himself. He had seen no men or women of Qui-Gon's age except for Wehutti. Even the other snipers had been elders, he realized. Were the mid-life people all working, or gathered somewhere for a meeting?

"Wehutti, where are all the middle-aged people?" Obi-Wan asked curiously.

"They're dead," Wehutti said flatly.

Even Qui-Gon looked startled. "The wars have wiped out the middle generation?"

"The *Daan* have wiped out the middle generation," Wehutti corrected grimly.

Obi-Wan had noticed the same lack of the middle generation in the Daan sector, but he didn't mention it to Wehutti. Obviously, the hatred of the Daan ran so deep in Wehutti that he could see no other sides of the story.

As they passed the blown-out café, Obi-Wan noticed graffiti on a partially destroyed wall. Scrawled in blazing red paint were the words THE YOUNG WILL RISE! WE ARE EVERYONE!

They turned a corner and walked through a neighborhood that had once prospered. As they made their way through the barricades onto once-pleasant squares, Obi-Wan noticed more graffiti. It all repeated what he'd seen on the café wall.

"Who are the Young?" he asked Wehutti, pointing to the graffiti. "Is it some organized group?"

Wehutti frowned. "Just kids, fooling around. It isn't enough that we have to live in Daan-destroyed homes and gardens. Our own children have to make our surroundings worse by defacing them. Ah, here we are."

He stopped in front of a once-luxurious mansion. A solid durasteel wall had been erected around it. It was topped with coils of electrowire. The windows were barred and Obi-Wan was sure they would release an electro-charge if touched. The house was now a fortress.

Wehutti stopped in front of the gate and pressed his eye against the iris-reader. The gate clicked open and he gestured for them to go inside.

They stepped into a walled courtyard. In front of the house was a rack filled with weapons.

"I'm afraid you must leave your lightsabers here," Wehutti said apologetically. He unstrapped his own weapons from their holsters. "This is Melida headquarters. It's a weapon-free zone."

Qui-Gon hesitated a fraction. Obi-Wan waited to see what he would do. A Jedi is never separated from his or her lightsaber.

"I'm sorry, but if you break this rule the negotiations will go badly for you," Wehutti said in a conciliatory tone. "They need proof of your trust since you ask for theirs. But it is your decision."

Slowly, Qui-Gon withdrew his lightsaber. He nodded at Obi-Wan to do the same. He slipped it into the rack, then took Obi-Wan's and slipped it next to his.

Wehutti smiled. "I'm sure this will go smoothly. This way."

Qui-Gon gestured for Obi-Wan to step in first as he gathered the folds of his cloak more closely around him. Wehutti followed directly behind them.

The hallway was dark, the stone floor pitted with holes. Wehutti led the way to a room on the left. Dark material was hung over the windows, shutting out any light. A lamp in one corner emitted a tiny glow that failed to chase away the shadows.

Obi-Wan made out a group of men and women sitting at a long table against the wall. They appeared to be waiting for them.

"The Melida Council," Wehutti explained to them in a whisper. "They rule the Melida people." He closed the heavy door behind them with a clang. Obi-Wan heard a lock spring. He glanced at Qui-Gon, trying to read if his Master felt the same jolt of apprehension.

"I have returned, comrades," Wehutti announced. He spread his arms to indicate Obi-Wan and Qui-Gon. "And I have brought two more Jedi hostages for our grand cause!"

CHAPTER 6

Wehutti had barely finished speaking when Qui-Gon moved. His lightsaber was activated and in his hand while the smile still beamed on Wehutti's face. Qui-Gon whirled, striking Wehutti on the shoulder. At the same time, he tossed Obi-Wan's lightsaber to him, hoping the boy was prepared to catch it.

Qui-Gon had been ready for Wehutti's betrayal. He did not need the Force to tell him that Wehutti had led them into a trap. His instincts had told him so before they had even reached the gates of the Inner Hub. When Wehutti had asked them to leave their weapons, Qui-Gon had only feigned his hesitation. He had foreseen the request and was already planning to get around it. It had been easy to unfurl his cloak to cover his recapture of the lightsabers. Even clever men can see only what they want to see. Wehutti had already been congratulating himself on his own ingenuity in luring the Jedi into his trap.

Wehutti fell with a cry of rage and pain. Obi-Wan activated his lightsaber.

"The door," Qui-Gon said to him, and prepared to defend himself against the group seated at the table. Several had half-risen, but the remaining Melida were still too shocked to react.

He heard Obi-Wan strike a blow to the lock. Two warriors, a man and a woman, had been quicker to react than the others. They started toward Qui-Gon, blasters in hand.

Suddenly, a light blazed on. Obi-Wan must have activated the lighting while he struggled with the door. It was better not to fight in the dark, though every Jedi is trained to be able to do so.

Qui-Gon suppressed a start of surprise when the Melida soldiers were fully revealed. All of them had already been severely wounded. He saw evidence of synth-flesh covering faces and exposed skin, as well as plastoid limbs. Two of the group wore breath-masks.

The Melida and the Daan were truly destroying each other, piece by piece.

This was only a fleeting thought, gone as quickly as it had come. Qui-Gon knew he must concentrate on the threat. He deflected the blaster fire as he ran to Obi-Wan, who had easily melted the lock. The door stood open. Obi-Wan and Qui-Gon raced from the room into the corridor.

Pounding footsteps overhead made them pause. A red light blinked insistently on the wall. Bars suddenly slammed down over the front door.

"Someone triggered a silent alarm," Qui-Gon said.

"We'll never get out that door," Obi-Wan warned.

They turned toward the hallway, racing to find a back exit. They knew they had little time before the rest of the Melida soldiers found them.

As they passed various points in the hallway, an electronic beep sounded.

"Those are location sensors," Qui-Gon said. "They're tracking us. They know exactly where we are."

At the end of the hallway they came to a heavily fortified door. Qui-Gon turned to the left and opened the first door he saw. They would have to get out a window if they could.

The room was high-ceilinged and full of stored equipment: circuits, nav-computers, sensor parts, dismantled droids.

Qui-Gon crossed to the window. Electro-bars ran in a grid over the pane. The security device would keep out life-forms and resist some forms of weaponry. But it was no match for a Jedi lightsaber. Qui-Gon cut through the bars with one swipe, leaving a gap big enough for them to leap through. Then he did the same with the window pane.

"Come, Padawan," he urged Obi-Wan.

The boy leaped easily through the gap. Qui-Gon followed. They found themselves in a walled and fortified courtyard. The wall would be easily scaled, Qui-Gon calculated. Too easily.

"Come on, Qui-Gon," Obi-Wan said impatiently.

"Wait." Qui-Gon walked closer to the wall. He crouched down and studied it. "It's mined," he told Obi-Wan. "Thermal detonators. If we climb it or even leap over it, the infrared sensors will blow us sky-high."

"So we're trapped."

"I'm afraid so," Qui-Gon answered, his mind sifting through the possibilities. They would have to reenter the Melida fortress and fight their way out. They didn't have much time. The soldiers would figure out where they were in seconds.

Qui-Gon whirled, his lightsaber raised, as he heard a metallic scraping sound. But no Melida warrior was in sight. He tracked the sound to the floor. A small sewer grate was being pushed back.

A small, dirty hand shot out of the opening and beckoned.

Obi-Wan looked at Qui-Gon, puzzled. "What should we do?" he whispered.

An ironic voice floated up from the grate. "Go ahead, talkdroids. Have a debate. I'll wait. We have plenty of time."

Qui-Gon heard shouting and running in the fortress. Any moment now, soldiers would appear at the window.

"Let's go," he told Obi-Wan.

He waited while his Padawan slithered into the opening. Qui-Gon followed blindly, his feet searching and finding the rung of a ladder leading downward. Hoping he hadn't made a mistake, Qui-Gon climbed down.

CHAPTER 7

Obi-Wan felt his way down the rickety metal ladder. He stepped off the last rung into ankle-deep water. Qui-Gon followed, moving with his usual grace, surprising for such a large man.

It was impossible to tell if their rescuer was a boy or a girl. The figure wore a hooded tunic, and pressed a dirty finger against its lips. Then he or she raised a finger and pointed above. The meaning was clear. If they weren't absolutely quiet, the guards above would hear.

The footsteps above were loud, the voices angry and insistent. The Jedi's rescuer turned and walked very slowly through the water, raising one foot and slipping it carefully back into the water so that no splash was heard. Obi-Wan followed the example. Softly, quietly, they moved farther down the tunnel.

The walls were shored up with splintered beams. Obi-Wan eyed them uneasily. The tunnel did not seem very secure to him. Still, it was an improvement over fighting his way out of a heavily armed fortress.

As soon as they had put some distance between themselves and the entrance, they picked up their pace. They walked through what felt like miles of tunnel, slogging through water and muck. Occasionally, the water was up to their knees. Their rescuer led them through old sewer tunnels, and the smell was terrible. Obi-Wan tried not to gag. Their rescuer seemed not to notice it, but kept up the same dogged, determined pace.

At last they came to a large vaulted space illuminated by several glow rods mounted on the walls. The ground was dry here, the air noticeably fresher. The room was dotted with rectangular stone boxes overgrown with moss. More lined the walls.

"Tombs," Qui-Gon murmured. "It's an old resting ground."

One of the tombs, scraped clean of moss, gave off a pale white gleam in the darkness. Stools were drawn up around it. A group of young boys and girls — some the same age as Obi-Wan, some younger — sat eating from bowls at the makeshift table.

A tall boy with close-cropped dark hair noticed their entrance. He stood.

"I found them," their rescuer announced.

The boy nodded. "Welcome, Jedi," he said solemnly. "We are the Young."

Around them, the walls seemed to move. Shapes took form and became boys and girls, appearing out of the shadows and from behind the tombs to gather around Obi-Wan and Qui-Gon.

Startled, Obi-Wan gazed around at their faces. Most of them were thin and dressed in rags. All wore makeshift weapons tied onto belts or shoulder holsters. They gazed at him curiously, without any attempt to be polite.

The tall boy moved forward. He wore a battered chestplate of plastoid armor. "I am Nield. I lead the Young. This is Cerasi."

Their rescuer threw back the hood, and Obi-Wan saw that she was a girl of about his age. Her copper hair was cut short and ragged. She had a small face with a pointed chin. Her pale green eyes were like crystals, glittering even in the dark vault.

"Thank you for rescuing us," Qui-Gon said. "Now, can you tell us why you did?"

"You would have been a pawn in the game of war," Nield said with a shrug. "We prefer that the game be over."

"I saw graffiti on walls about the Young," Obi-Wan said. "Are you Melida or Daan?"

Cerasi shook her head. "We are everyone," she said, lifting her chin proudly.

"And you want the war to stop?" Qui-Gon asked.

"There is a cease-fire," Obi-Wan pointed out.

Nield waved his hand. "The war will start again. Tomorrow, next week—it always does. Even the oldest among the elders don't remember what the original grievance was. They don't remember why the war began. They only remember the battles. They keep archives and go once a week to remind each other of the blood that has been spilled. They used to make us go, too."

"The Halls of Evidence," Obi-Wan said, nodding.

"Yes, they pour money into those halls while the cities decay around us," Nield said contemptuously. "While the children starve and the ill die for lack of med supplies. Both Melida and Daan use up huge tracts of land while there is no land left to farm, no land left that has not been scarred by war or taken up by the preparation for more war."

"Yet they go on fighting," Cerasi put in. "The hatred never stops."

"And who do our glorious leaders defend?" Nield asked. "Only the dead." He gestured at the tombs. "The dead are everywhere on Melida/

Daan. We have no spaces left to put them. This is an old burial ground, and there are many others above us. The Young are for the living. It is up to us to take back the planet. The middle generation is gone — our parents are dead. Any who are left have joined with the elders to keep on fighting. Right now the tactics are sniping and sabotage, since most of the weaponry and ammunition were depleted in the last great battle."

"There are hardly any starfighters left," Cerasi told them. "Both the Melida and the Daan are pouring whatever money they have into factories to make more weapons. They are forcing children to work in them. They are forcing anyone over fourteen to join the army. That's why we came underground. It was either this or die."

Obi-Wan gazed around the vault at the faces of the boys and girls around him. From what he had seen in his short time on the planet, he knew that Nield and Cerasi were right. The elders were destroying the planet. The time-honored moral law of improving a world for future generations did not hold here. Even children were sacrificed to hatred. Obi-Wan admired them for fighting back.

"That's why we saved you from Wehutti," Nield explained. "The War Council was planning to use the two of you as hostages to force the Jedi Council to back a Melida government.

They hoped to force you to speak on their behalf in the Senate on Coruscant."

"Then he does not know the Jedi," Qui-Gon remarked.

A slender boy spoke up. "He doesn't know anything," he said in a joking tone. "He's a Melida."

Nield sprang forward like a shot from a blaster rifle. He wrapped two hands around the boy's neck and picked him up off the floor. The boy's feet flailed out as Nield squeezed his throat. The boy's eyes widened in a desperate plea. He let out an anguished croaking noise, trying to get air into his lungs. Nield squeezed harder.

Qui-Gon took a step forward, but at that moment Nield loosened his grip. The boy fell to the floor, gasping.

"No talk like that here," Nield said. "*Ever.* We are everyone. Towan, you'll sleep for three days in Drain Two for that."

The boy nodded, his hands on his throat protectively, trying to gasp in air. No one looked at him as he slinked to the back of the group and disappeared into the shadows.

"We will help you locate Tahl," Nield said, calmly returning to the conversation as though nothing had happened. "But you must help us, too."

Obi-Wan had to stop himself from crying out, *Of course we will help you!* It was up to his Master to do that. Never in any mission had he met a cause that seemed so just. They had been sent here to rescue Tahl, but surely if they could continue her mission as guardian of peace they should do so. It was in the galaxy's best interest to stabilize the planet. Nield was offering them a chance to do this as well as their primary mission. He waited for Qui-Gon to speak. All the faces in the vault turned expectantly to the tall, rugged Jedi Knight.

"We have spoken to the Melida," Qui-Gon said cautiously. "We have spoken to you. But we have not received a complete picture of what goes on here. I cannot promise you help until I have seen something of the Daan."

It took a moment for Qui-Gon's words to sink in. Then Nield's face flushed with anger. "You want to see something of the Daan?" he asked challengingly. "I am a Daan. Come with me. I'll show you that the Daan are no better than the Melida. And no worse."

CHAPTER 8

Cerasi led the way through the tunnels again, away from the direction they had come in, straight into Daan territory.

"Cerasi knows every step of these tunnels," Nield explained as they followed behind her. His earlier anger had passed as quickly as it had come. "She was the first to come down here to live."

"Why did she leave her life above ground?" Qui-Gon asked.

"She saw the way things are, as I did," Nield answered. "There is no life for us up there. Down here we have muck and filth, but we have hope." His teeth gleamed in the darkness as he smiled. "It may seem strange to you, but we're happier here."

"It's not strange at all," Obi-Wan said.

"Was it the Young who shored up the tunnels?" Qui-Gon asked. "The work seems recent."

Nield nodded before squeezing through a small opening, then waited for them to enter the new tunnel. "We did it bit by bit, piece by piece. The tunnels were built during the Eighteenth Battle of Zehava. The Daan expanded the water and sewage tunnels and broke through into the underground burial vaults from the Tenth War, working secretly at night to enter the Melida sector. That's when the city was divided between north and south. They won that battle."

"And then the Nineteenth Battle of Zehava was fought barely six months later," Cerasi said, overhearing them. "The battles never stop. They never will, unless we act."

Cerasi paused. Light filtered down from a crack in the stone overhead. "Here."

Qui-Gon eyed the curved ceiling of the tunnel. "Where?"

Cerasi unclipped a ring of tension cord from her belt. She expertly tossed the cord above and, with a flicking motion of her wrist, wrapped it around a hook embedded in the mortar of the ceiling. Cerasi tested it, then glanced at Qui-Gon and flashed him a grin. "Don't worry, it will even hold *you*."

She scrambled up the cord, hand over hand.

When she had almost reached the top, she swung out from the cord and hooked her fingers into the crack in the stone. She remained there, pressing her face against the crack.

"All clear," she called down softly. She pushed off and swung hard, tilting her body back until she was almost upside down. Using her momentum, she kicked at the stone with her feet. It dislodged, and with her next swing, she gave it a more gentle kick to move it out of the way. Qui-Gon heard a thud as the stone hit the ground overhead. On her next swing, Cerasi easily hooked her feet into the opening, then bent her body to swing herself out.

The whole operation had taken maybe thirty seconds. Qui-Gon admired Cerasi's agility and strength.

She popped her head back down. "Nothing to it."

One by one, the remaining three pulled themselves up the cord and then swung out of the opening. They were not quite as graceful and swift as Cerasi, but they made it.

Qui-Gon found himself in a storeroom located in a service building in back of an abandoned estate. It was a clever place to hide an entrance to the tunnels.

Now Nield led the way, since he was familiar with the Daan sector. "Don't worry," he told the

Jedi. "I'm a Daan, and many know me here. You're safer in Daan territory. At least the Daan don't want to take you hostage."

Now that Qui-Gon had more time, he was able to study the Daan sector more closely. It didn't seem that much different than the Inner Hub. Abandoned, bombed-out buildings. Barricades. Food shortages in the shops. And everywhere people going about their daily lives with old and ragged weapons strapped to chests, hips, and ankles. He did not see many faces younger than sixty or older than twenty.

"This used to be a beautiful city," Nield remarked, sadness in his voice. "I've seen drawings and hologram recreations. It's been completely rebuilt seven times. When I was very young, I remember trees and blossoms and even a museum that had nothing to do with the dead."

"There were no barricades for five years," Cerasi said softly. "Daans and Melidas mixed in both sectors. In some neighborhoods they even lived side by side. Then the Twenty-Fifth Battle of Zehava began."

"What about your parents, Cerasi?" Obi-Wan asked.

Cerasi's expression was hard for Qui-Gon to read. She seemed to struggle with the decision to share even a part of her story. "Their hatred destroyed them, like so many others. My mother died while conducting a sniper raid. My brother was sent to the country to work in a munitions factory. I have not heard a word from him since."

"And your father?"

Cerasi's face smoothed out, became bland. "He is dead," she said colorlessly.

A story there, Qui-Gon thought. Each of the Young, he realized, would have a similar one, full of sorrow and tragedy, of parents lost too soon, families fractured. That was the bond between them.

Ahead, Qui-Gon saw a glimpse of blue water. They walked down a wide boulevard, leaping over large holes where proton torpedoes had fallen.

"This is Lake Weir," Nield said. "I used to come swimming here when I was little. Now you'll see what the Daan have done."

As they drew closer, the patch of blue Qui-Gon had glimpsed between two buildings widened, and he could see that the lake was quite large. It would have been a beautiful expanse, except for the low, massive ebony stone building that floated slightly above the water by repulsor-posts.

"Another Hall of Evidence," Nield said, disgusted. "This was the last remaining body of water within a thousand kilometers. Now no one can enjoy it but the dead."

The wind ruffled Nield's hair as he gazed at the scene. His disgusted look softened to one of sadness, and Qui-Gon imagined that a memory of one of those swims had surfaced. He was suddenly struck by how young Nield looked. Underground, his manner had made him seem older than Obi-Wan, but they were about the same age.

Qui-Gon gave a quick glance at Cerasi. Her slender, pretty face was pale, almost drawn, but he could still see the young child she'd once been. They were all so young, he thought in sorrow. Too young for the task they'd set themselves — to right centuries of wrong, to save a world cracked by tension and strife.

"Come," Nield said. "Let's see the happy dead speak."

He strode forward, and they followed. He entered the stone door and walked quickly down the aisles, past monument after monument. He activated hologram after hologram but did not stop to hear their tales. Their voices filled the huge chamber, echoing with their stories of revenge and hatred. Nield began to run, pressing globe after globe to activate the ghosts.

Finally, he stopped in front of the last hologram he'd activated. It was a tall man with shoulder-length hair, wearing armor.

"I am Micae, son of Terandi of Garth, from the North Country," the hologram said. "I was but a boy when the Melida invaded Garth and herded my people into camps. There, many died, including —"

"And why did the Melida do that, you fool?" Nield mocked the figure, drowning out the list of the dead. "Perhaps because the Daan soldiers in the North Country attacked the Melida settlements without warning, killing hundreds?"

The warrior's tale went on. "— and my mother died that day without ever being reunited with my father. My father died in the great Battle of the Plains, avenging the great wrong of the Melida during the Battle of the North —"

"— Which had taken place a century before!" Nield scoffed.

"— and today I go to battle with my three sons. My youngest son is too young to join us. I fight today so that he may never have to fight —"

"Fat chance!" Nield jeered.

"We seek justice, not vengeance. And that is why I know we shall triumph." The warrior raised his fist, then opened it in a gesture of peace.

"Liars and fools!" Nield shouted. He turned

abruptly away from the hologram. "Let's get out of here. I can't bear their stupid voices any more."

They walked out into the open air. Gray clouds were massing overhead, and the water looked almost as black as the great hall that floated above it, casting a long shadow. It was hard to tell where the building ended and the water began.

"Do you see?" Nield demanded of Qui-Gon. "They will never stop. The Young are this world's only hope. I know the Jedi are wise. You must see that our cause is just. Don't we deserve a chance?"

Nield's golden eyes burned with fervor. Qui-Gon glanced at Obi-Wan. He saw that the boy had been not only moved by Nield's words, but deeply stirred.

That made him uneasy. Though a Jedi's heart could be touched, it was his duty to remain unbiased and calm. The situation here was complicated and volatile. They would need clear heads to navigate it. His instinct told him it was better not to take sides.

But there was the question of Tahl. Rescue was their primary mission. Nield had promised his help. Could he deliver on his promise?

"I know where Tahl is being held," Nield said,

almost as though he'd read Qui-Gon's mind. "She is alive."

"You can get us to this place?" Qui-Gon asked.

"Cerasi can," Nield said. "It is heavily guarded. But I have a plan to take care of that. While you are rescuing Tahl, the Young will launch a surprise attack."

"I am not sure how surprising an attack would be, given that the Melida know that the Jedi are on the loose," Qui-Gon said. "They will be expecting it."

"But they will not be expecting a *Daan* attack."

"Are the Daan planning to attack?" Obi-Wan asked.

"No," Nield answered. "But that doesn't mean the Melida can't *think* they are. Our plan is to stage diversionary attacks in both the Melida and Daan sectors. The Melida will think that the Daan are attacking and send their forces out into the streets to defend themselves. The Daan will do the same. I promise you confusion and chaos. Then you can go after Tahl."

"But you have no weapons," Obi-Wan said. "How do you expect to attack?"

"We have a plan," Nield said mysteriously. "All we ask of you is to stay in the vault and not contact the Melida. Right now they are searching for you everywhere. It is better that their forces be busy with that chore so that we can do our work."

"So you see how easy we're making this for you?" Cerasi asked. "All we ask is that you do nothing."

"We'll take care of the diversion," Nield continued. "You take care of Tahl. I also know that her wounds were severe. She needs medical attention."

Annoyed, Qui-Gon gazed out at the water to buy time. He knew Nield was blackmailing him, forcing him to bend to his wishes so that Qui-Gon could fulfill his mission. He had been outmaneuvered by a child.

And Obi-Wan, he saw, was enjoying it. Another curl of apprehension registered along his spine.

He turned back to Nield and Cerasi. "All right," he said. "Obi-Wan and I will wait for you to bring us to Tahl. Our primary objective is her rescue. After that, you're on your own. Is that good enough?"

Nield grinned. "It is all we need."

CHAPTER 9

Back at the tunnel, preparations began. Nield and Cerasi huddled with the rest of the Young, deep in conversation. Obi-Wan sat quietly at the table, watching them. The determination on their faces told him that whatever the outcome, the Daan and the Melida were both in for a big surprise at dawn the next day.

Qui-Gon paced on the other side of the room, displaying a rare show of impatience.

"If you need help with strategy —" he began.

Cerasi turned. "No," she said curtly. "We don't need any help."

"Another opinion can only strengthen your odds," Qui-Gon said quietly.

This time, Cerasi didn't bother to turn. Nield did not even look up.

"We do not *want* your help, Jedi," Cerasi said, even more sharply than before.

Obi-Wan glanced at Qui-Gon to gauge his reaction. He saw his Master struggle with his irritation. But although Qui-Gon could be impulsive, he was never petty. The irritation left him, and his usual mask of calm returned.

"Padawan, I am going to explore the tunnels," he told Obi-Wan in a low voice. "It is better not to rely totally on the Young to guide us. You remain here."

Obi-Wan nodded. For once, he didn't want to accompany Qui-Gon. He wanted to stay and watch the Young plan the battle.

Cerasi divided the young people into teams and assigned them tasks. They worked on makeshift weapons fashioned from scraps. Their most prominent weapon was a powerful slingshot that threw laserballs. The balls could only sting a life-form if they connected, but if they hit a hard object, they made a sound like blaster fire.

Over the course of the afternoon, Obi-Wan tried to grow used to the muffled sound of explosions. War toys were part of the childhood of both Melida and Daan. The Young were modifying them to amplify their sound effects. They worked in the rooms branching off the main tunnel on missile tubes, packing them with pebbles and paint.

Cerasi worked on a pile of slingshots in a corner, honing them with a sharp knife and testing their accuracy with wadded up flimsiplast. The flimsiplast winged across the high space, hitting the same stone block with deadly accuracy. Cerasi worked tirelessly, without a break.

"I'd like to help," Obi-Wan said, approaching her. "Not with strategy," he added quickly. "I know you have that under control. But I *can* help with this."

Cerasi pushed a lock of hair from her eyes and smiled slightly. "I guess I was hard on your Boss-Master, huh?"

"He's not my boss, really," Obi-Wan said. "That's not the Jedi way. He's more of a guide."

"Sure, whatever you say. But if you ask me, elders always think they know best. They just get in the way." She handed a knife to Obi-Wan. "If you can hone it to the same thickness as the ones I did, we could get these done in a flash."

Obi-Wan sat and began to scrape the knife against the supple wood. "What do you think our chances of success are tomorrow?"

"Excellent," Cerasi said firmly. "We're relying on the hatred of the two sectors. All we need to do is create the *illusion* of battle. Both sides will react without bothering to verify reports of blaster fire and torpedo launches. They expect warfare at any moment."

"Your battle may be an illusion, but the danger is not," Obi-Wan pointed out. "Both sides will have real weapons to fire."

Cerasi shook her head. "I'm not afraid."

"Awareness of fear can protect you if it does not overtake you," Obi-Wan replied.

Cerasi snorted. "Is that one of your Boss-Master's Jedi sayings?"

Obi-Wan flushed. "Yes. And I have found it to be true. Awareness of fear is an instinct that warns you to be careful. Anyone going into battle who says they are not afraid is a fool."

"Well, call me a fool, Pada-Jedi," Cerasi said flatly. "I'm not afraid."

"Ah," Obi-Wan said lightly. "You go into glorious battle without fear, confident that your filthy enemy will collapse."

He was repeating the vain boasts of the dead in the Halls of Evidence, and Cerasi knew it. She flushed as Obi-Wan had a moment before.

"More Jedi wisdom. It's a wonder you manage to survive this long, if you keep pointing out what foolish things people say," Cerasi finally said with a half smile. "Okay, I get your point. I'm no better than my ancestors, marching blindly into a battle I will lose."

"I'm not saying you will lose."

Cerasi paused, fully seeing Obi-Wan for the first time. "Well, maybe I'll feel afraid on the day of the battle. But today I feel ready. This is the first step toward justice. I can't wait to take it. Do you have any wisdom about that?"

"No," Obi-Wan admitted. Cerasi was unlike anyone he'd ever met before. "Justice is something to fight for. If I didn't believe that, I wouldn't be a Jedi."

Cerasi put down her slingshot. "Being a Jedi is as much a part of you as being part of the Young is to me," she observed, her crystal green eyes studying him. "I guess the difference is that the Young don't have any guides. We guide ourselves."

"Being an apprentice is a journey that is an honor to undertake," Obi-Wan replied. But he feared his words were weak. He was used to saying them and believing them with his whole heart. Being a Jedi was at the core of him. But in just a few hours with the Young, he had seen a commitment that had confused him as much as it had stirred him.

Of course, he had seen deep commitment at the Temple among the Jedi students. But with some students, there often seemed to be pride mixed in. They were the elite, picked out of millions to be trained.

Whenever Yoda saw pride in a Jedi student, he found ways to expose it and put the student on the right path. Pride was often based in arrogance, and had no place in a Jedi. Part of the Jedi training was to eliminate pride and substitute sureness and humility. The Force only flourished in those who knew they were connected to all life-forms.

Here in the tunnels, Obi-Wan saw a pureness he had only glimpsed in his talks with Yoda, or his observance of Qui-Gon. That pureness was in people his own age. They did not have to strive for it. They possessed it. Perhaps because the cause they believed in was more than a concept in their minds. It was bred in their blood and bones, born in their suffering.

He felt defensive, as though Cerasi had attacked his dedication to the Jedi way. "Nield is the leader of the Young," he pointed out. "So you, too, have a boss."

"Nield is the best at strategy," Cerasi said. "If we didn't have someone to organize us, we would fall apart."

"And someone to punish you?" Obi-Wan asked, remembering how Nield had almost strangled a boy.

Cerasi hesitated. Her voice softened as she continued. "Nield may seem harsh to you, but he has to be. Hatred was taught to us before we could walk. We have to be firm to stamp it out. Our vision of a new world can only survive if our hatred dies. We must forget everything we were taught. We must begin again. Nield knows this better than anyone. Perhaps because he's had it harder than any of us here."

"In what way?" Obi-Wan asked.

Cerasi sighed. She put down the slingshot she'd been working on. "That last hologram he triggered — the one he mocked — was Nield's father. He went into battle with Nield's three brothers. They all died. Nield was five years old. One month later his mother made preparations to be part of the next great battle. She left him with a cousin, a young girl who was more like a sister to him. His mother went off to fight, and she was killed, too. Then the Melida invaded his village. His cousin escaped and took him to Zehava. He had a few peaceful years, but then the Daan attacked the Melida sector, and his cousin had to fight. She was seventeen, old enough then. She died, too. Nield was left on the streets to fend for himself. He was eight years old. There were those who tried to care for him. He wouldn't live with anyone, but he did take shelter and food when he needed it. He didn't want to depend on anyone ever again. Can you blame him?"

Obi-Wan pictured all those people who loved Nield — all of them dying, one after the other. "No," he said softly. "I don't blame him at all."

Cerasi sighed. "The point is, I was raised to think of the Daan as beasts, barely human. Nield was the first Daan I knew. He was the one who united both the Daan and the Melida orphans. He walked into the care centers and gathered them up, promised them freedom and peace. Then he made sure they had it. If they had stayed in the care center, eventually they'd be taken in a sweep."

"A sweep?" Obi-Wan asked.

"Both Melida and Daan rely on the orphaned children for factory work or conscription, if they're old enough," Cerasi said flatly. "They either work or fight. It's easy to find them in the city care centers. In the towns and villages, the children just run away."

"Where do they go?"

Cerasi frowned. "They live off the land and scavenge. There are whole tribes of children beyond the city's walls. Nield has worked hard to organize them, too. They keep in contact with stolen comlinks. They don't want any more war." Cerasi turned to him. "So you ask me what our chances of success will be, and I know I answered you. But truly, I can't even think of chances or odds. We will succeed because we have to. Our world is becoming a wasteland, Obi-Wan. Only we can stop it."

Obi-Wan nodded. He felt himself beginning to understand Cerasi. He saw that her brusqueness masked deep feeling.

"We could use your help, though," Cerasi went on. "You have ties to the Jedi Council, and they have ties to Coruscant. You can show the entire galaxy that our cause is just. Jedi support means everything."

"Cerasi, I can't promise you Jedi support," Obi-Wan said quietly. Surprising himself, he put his hand over hers. "I can only promise you mine."

Her bright gaze held his. "Why don't you come with Nield and me tomorrow? We're doing the first raid into Daan territory."

Obi-Wan hesitated. As a Jedi apprentice, he would be breaking the rules if he agreed without asking Qui-Gon's permission. But if he asked, Qui-Gon would most likely refuse.

He had already broken the rules by pledging his own support to Cerasi and her cause. That promise could conflict with the Jedi mission.

But he couldn't help himself. The cause of the Young spoke directly and urgently to his heart. As a Jedi, he didn't fight for his own family, his own world, or his own people. He fought for what Yoda and the Council — and Qui-Gon — decided he should fight for.

Cerasi and Nield had defined their own struggle. Obi-Wan was struck with a pang of deep envy for them. He had spent so much time with those older than himself. He had listened so often to their wisdom. Now he felt welcomed back into something different. He could be a part of a community here — he hadn't realized how much he missed a community of boys and girls his own age.

Cerasi's hand felt warm beneath his own. Her fingers were slender and delicate. Suddenly they intertwined with his and squeezed, and he felt their strength.

"Will you come?" she asked.

"Yes," he said. "I will."

CHAPTER 10

That night, the Young rolled sleeping quilts onto the tombs. Qui-Gon found an open space near one of the adjacent tunnel entrances, where the air was fresh.

Obi-Wan approached him awkwardly. "Nield and Cerasi have asked me to share their quarters," he said. "They watch over the youngest children."

Qui-Gon gave him a questioning look, but he nodded. "Sleep well, Padawan."

Obi-Wan picked up a sleeping quilt and returned to Nield and Cerasi. They slept in a small anteroom off the vault. Nield put a finger to his lips as Obi-Wan entered.

"The children are asleep," he whispered. "We should be sleeping as well. We'll need all our rest for tomorrow." He put his hand on Obi-

Wan's forearm. "Cerasi told me you will join us. I'm honored."

"It is my honor to help you," Obi-Wan answered.

He settled himself on the floor next to Nield and Cerasi. He thought he wouldn't be able to sleep, but the children's quiet breathing lulled him.

It was hard to tell what time it was when he awoke. Cerasi rose from her sleeping area and leaned over Nield to touch his shoulder. Nield was already awake and stood immediately.

Obi-Wan stood as well. He was ready. He was acting not as a Jedi, but as a person — a friend. He grabbed his lightsaber and the slingshot Cerasi had given him the night before. There was an entrance from the anteroom directly into the tunnel toward Daan. Qui-Gon wouldn't see him leave.

Obi-Wan knew he was wrong not to ask permission, but he wasn't sure how angry Qui-Gon would be when he discovered he was gone. After all, Qui-Gon himself had offered to help with strategy for the battle.

Obi-Wan was glad he'd made the decision as he joined Nield and Cerasi on the deserted streets of the Daan-controlled Outer Circle. The three moved as one unit in the chilly early morning air. They walked purposefully down the deserted streets, their soft footfalls barely making a sound. Nield and Cerasi had already decided on their first targets.

They shimmied up a pipe and climbed onto the roof of a dwelling. From here, they could see the sun, more a suggestion of gathering light than a source of radiance.

"I hate to wake everybody up," Nield said, flashing a grin.

"It's time they were out of bed anyway." Cerasi held up a toy missile tube. "I'm ready."

Obi-Wan had clipped various projectiles onto his belt. He stuffed one into the missile tube. The projectiles had been fashioned around tiny amplifiers so that the sound they made when they hit would mimic the sound of a real proton missile. Cerasi and Nield had chosen a street that would echo the sound.

"Let's go," Obi-Wan agreed.

Cerasi aimed the toy missile at the abandoned building across the street. She fired.

The loud sound of the explosion surprised them.

"Listen to that. It worked!" Nield exulted.

He fit a laserball into his slingshot and fired at the wall across the street. The unmistakable *ping ping ping* of blaster fire erupted. Obi-Wan quickly stuffed another projectile into the tube and Cerasi shot it off. The *blam* echoed off the building fronts below.

Nield continued to shoot laserballs from his slingshot, and Obi-Wan followed suit. They shot ball after ball, reloading and firing rapidly. The sound of blaster fire echoed down the street. Someone emerged from a door across the way and looked up and down the street quickly. Nield and Obi-Wan shot a rain of laserballs into an abandoned building, where no one would see them land.

Crackcrackcrack! The laserballs hit the solid surface, making an even louder sound. The Daan quickly ducked back into the building.

"He'll sound an alert," Nield said. "We're done here. Let's go."

Jumping from building to building, they made their way to another quiet street. They repeated the procedure, then moved on. Racing now, they fired down randomly with laserballs while Cerasi shot projectiles where their explosive sound would echo the most. While they moved from block to block, they shifted barricades where they could to block any military vehicles. At checkpoints, they rained their false weapon-fire over the heads of the guards, who took defensive postures, sweeping the empty streets with infrared electrobinoculars to look for the unseen attackers.

The sun rose, and sirens began to sound over the city. Nield turned to them. The rising sun reflected red off his dark hair. "Now for military headquarters."

Excitement coursed through Obi-Wan. It was almost like a game, this ruse that Nield and Cerasi had concocted. But now the game would get serious. Hitting a military target, even with fake explosives, would be dangerous.

Nield led the way across the rooftops to the Daan military headquarters. From the roof of a building across the street, Obi-Wan could see soldiers running toward landspeeders, carrying blasters and torpedo launchers. Obviously, they were hurrying to investigate the many alarms that had sprung up.

"So far, so good," Cerasi breathed. "There won't be as many soldiers around."

This part would be tricky. They would not be firing at houses full of sleeping civilians. The military would react swiftly. But Nield had pointed out that if they did not convince the military that an attack had been launched, their plan wouldn't work. If the military thought they were under fire as well, they might conclude that this was not random sniper fire, but a full-scale attack.

In addition to Nield, Cerasi, and Obi-Wan, other groups of the Young should have been heading out to other Daan and Melida neighborhoods. Their attacks would be launched simultaneously with the attack on military headquarters.

They waited until the soldiers had taken off in their speeders. Two guards stood outside behind transparent armored shields. Cerasi loaded her beam tube. Obi-Wan and Nield placed laserballs in their slingshots. On the whispered count of three from Cerasi, they fired.

The laserballs hit the building, sounding like blaster fire. The projectile boomed. Already, the three had loaded and shot again, then quickly scuttled back on their hands and knees and ran to the edge of the roof to jump to the adjoining building. They fired again.

Soldiers streamed out of the building in full plastoid armor, blasters in hand. Electro-binoculars were trained on the street and buildings above. Armored plates rattled down over windows and doors. A siren blasted insistently. Soldiers began to spread out down the street. Floaters took off for air surveillance. Armored vehicles poured out from an underground holding station.

"It's time to get out of here," Cerasi said.

Stuffing the toys and slingshots into their belts, they dashed across the rooftop and quickly shimmied down a drainpipe. When they hit the street, they slowed their pace, trying to look like Daan teenagers out for a morning walk.

"You there! Halt!"

They froze. The voice had come from behind them. Nield had already given them identity cards, so they thought they'd be able to pass. Cerasi slipped a package out of her tunic. Obi-Wan glanced at her, puzzled. Did she have a weapon? Of course, he had his lightsaber, but he would never be able to take on the troops swarming over the streets. He would only endanger Cerasi and Nield.

They turned and saw three soldiers approaching them, blasters aimed straight at their hearts.

"Identity cards," one soldier said in a clipped tone. Quickly, the three handed them over. Nield had given Obi-Wan a disc from a Daan boy who was his age and weight. The soldiers inserted the discs into a readout machine. Obi-Wan waited for them to hand them back, but instead, the first soldier gave a look at the other two to keep them. He was still suspicious. He gave Nield, Cerasi, and Obi-Wan a hard look.

"Is there anything wrong?" Nield asked worriedly.

"What do you have there?" The first soldier pointed at Cerasi's package with his blaster.

"M-muja muffins," Cerasi stammered nervously. She held out the package. "For breakfast. We go every morning."

"Let me see." The soldier opened the top of the package. Inside, Obi-Wan saw a row of muffins wrapped in napkins.

"What's on your belts?" the other soldier asked. "Aren't you a little old for toys?"

"We're practicing for the army," Nield answered. He lifted his chin. "We can't wait to fight the filthy Melida."

"What's that?" the soldier pointed to Obi-Wan's lightsaber.

Obi-Wan held it up and activated it. "The newest toy on Gala. My grandfather sells them over on Victory Street."

The soldiers eyed it. "We never had toys like that when we were young," the first said ruefully.

"In the next battle of Zehava, the Daan will prevail!" Obi-Wan answered, waving his lightsaber.

"We might be in the next battle of Zehava right now, so hurry along and take shelter," the third soldier said gruffly. He handed Nield back his identity card and motioned for the other soldiers to do the same. "You may be fighting with real weapons before long."

The three soldiers marched off, their com-links crackling with reports of more attacks in the city.

"That was close," Cerasi breathed. "I'm glad I brought those muja muffins. It gave us a reason to be on the street so early."

"And I thought you brought them in case I was hungry," Obi-Wan managed to tease. His heartbeat was returning to normal. He didn't want to think about how Qui-Gon would have reacted if he had been captured by the Daan.

"That was a smart move, to activate that lightsaber and call it a toy," Nield said to Obi-Wan. "Lucky for you they were too dumb to realize you were a Jedi."

Cerasi eyed him. "I have a feeling Obi-Wan was ready to use it."

Nield grinned broadly. "I have a feeling he can save us all."

The three laughed together in relief. Obi-Wan felt a current run between himself and Cerasi and Nield. Even though he was still in danger, he had never felt so free.

CHAPTER 11

Qui-Gon sat in the shadows, watching the furious activity of the Young as they dashed in and out of the vault for supplies, then hurried out to return to the streets above.

Something had woken him before dawn, a soft flurry of movement. He had seen Obi-Wan leave with Cerasi and Nield. He had let his Padawan go.

It would have been easy to step forward and challenge Obi-Wan. Qui-Gon's anger had surged, and he had wanted to confront the boy. Obi-Wan had no right to leave without permission. He had violated Qui-Gon's trust. It was a small violation, but it stung.

He and Obi-Wan had not yet achieved the perfect mind-communion of the Master-Padawan relationship. They had merely taken a few steps on a long journey together. They occasionally had disagreements and misunderstandings. But

Obi-Wan had never deliberately concealed something from him before.

Obviously, Obi-Wan was afraid that Qui-Gon would not let him go. The boy was right; he would have forbidden it. Qui-Gon believed the Young sincerely wanted peace, but he wasn't sure if they would follow through with their good intentions if they gained any sort of power. He saw much anger in them. Obi-Wan saw only passion.

At last Nield, Cerasi, and Obi-Wan returned. Qui-Gon let out a slow breath of relief. He had started to worry.

"Time for phase two," Nield said as the three entered the vault. "We go for the weapon storage of both sides."

"What about Tahl?" Qui-Gon asked.

"Cerasi will lead you to Tahl," Nield said. "Deila?"

A tall, slender girl paused as she loaded more projectiles into pouches that hung from her belt. "Yes?"

"How's it going on the Melida side?"

She grinned. "Chaos. They think the Daan are everywhere, even in their closets."

"Good." Nield turned back to Qui-Gon. "There should be enough confusion for you to slip through. Cerasi will bring you, but you'll have to rescue Tahl on your own."

"That's fine," Qui-Gon agreed. He didn't want to put the girl in danger.

Obi-Wan didn't meet his Master's gaze as the two Jedi followed Cerasi into a narrow tunnel that led off the vault. Qui-Gon pushed his anger aside. He would not confront Obi-Wan about sneaking out. Not yet. He turned his mind to the task ahead. He had to focus on Tahl now.

Cerasi led them through a maze of tunnels until they came to a grate. Pale gray light filtered down.

"We are underneath the building where Tahl is being held," she whispered. "This will lead you to a lower level of a military barracks. Tahl is being held in a room three doors to the right. There will be guards there, but probably not as many as there were before. Every soldier is needed on the streets."

"How many were there before?" Qui-Gon asked in a low murmur.

"That's the bad news," Cerasi said ruefully. "She's guarded by only two guards, but right around the corner is the main quarters for soldiers. It's where they come to eat and sleep. So there are always plenty of soldiers walking back and forth. That's why Nield and I figured you needed a diversion." She pointed overhead. "The grate leads directly into a grain storage area, so you can climb up without being seen."

"Thank you, Cerasi," Qui-Gon said quietly. "We can find our own way back."

But when Qui-Gon and Obi-Wan emerged into a small storage area crowded with sacks of grain, Cerasi's head popped up out of the grate after them.

"I thought you were going back," Obi-Wan whispered.

She grinned. "I have a feeling you'll need my help." She dangled her slingshot. "A diversion might come in handy."

Obi-Wan returned her grin, but Qui-Gon frowned. "I don't want to put you in danger, Cerasi. This is not part of our deal. Nield said —"

"I make my own decisions, Qui-Gon," Cerasi interrupted. "I'm offering my help. I know the layout. Will you accept my offer or not?" Cerasi's chin stuck out challengingly. Her crystal eyes glinted at Qui-Gon.

"All right," he said. "But if Obi-Wan and I get in trouble, you leave. Do you promise me?"

"I promise," Cerasi agreed.

Qui-Gon eased the door open a crack and surveyed the area. A long hallway was lined with heavy metal doors. One soldier hurried down the hall and disappeared around a turning. Two soldiers were posted as guards outside one of the doors. It was where Tahl was being held.

A soldier headed toward him, moving fast. Qui-Gon faded back, but kept close to the opening.

"Going back out there?" one of the guards asked.

"We've got an invasion on our hands," the soldier said curtly. "Just got news of an attack only two blocks away. I've got to find my unit."

The guards exchanged nervous glances. "We're sitting ducks in here," the first one muttered. "We should be out there fighting. This duty is a waste of time anyway. I don't care if she is a Jedi, she's too weak to be a threat."

"She's done for," the other guard said. "It won't be long."

Rage and pain rose in Qui-Gon. It couldn't be too late. He controlled the anger and called on the Force to help him. He knew Obi-Wan was doing the same, for the Force was suddenly a presence in the room, surging around them.

"Qui-Gon," Cerasi whispered. "I have an idea. Will you listen?"

"Do I have a choice?" Qui-Gon responded.

Cerasi moved closer and whispered her plan in his ear.

"All right," he said. "But then you leave. Agreed?"

Cerasi nodded. Then she eased open the door and slipped out.

It took a moment for the guards to notice her.

Cerasi hurried toward them, her expression stricken.

"Halt!" the guards called.

"What?" Cerasi asked, distracted. She kept on moving.

"Halt or we'll shoot!" the guards warned.

Cerasi stopped. She wrung her hands together. "But my father is here! I have to see him!"

"Who is your father?"

Cerasi drew herself up. "Wehutti, the great hero. I must tell him that my aunt Sonie is dead. She was blown up by a foul Daan proton grenade. You must let me pass!"

"You are Wehutti's daughter?"

"Yes, look. I have an identity card." Cerasi showed the guards her Melida card.

One of the guards took it, then swiped it down his readout. When he handed it back to her, his voice was kind.

"I haven't seen Wehutti here. He's most likely on the streets. We're being invaded, you know."

"You think I don't know that?" Cerasi cried. "The Daan are taking the Hub block by block. They'll be here any minute. I need my father! He promised he'd be here if I needed him. He promised!" Cerasi's voice wobbled. With her slight figure and her quavering voice, she seemed younger than she was.

The guards exchanged a glance. "All right. But then you've got to clear out and seek shelter," the second one said.

Cerasi hurried down the hall and turned the corner. A moment passed, then another. Qui-Gon waited patiently. He had confidence in Cerasi. She would need time to circle around to the other side of the guards.

Suddenly, the sound of blaster fire echoed down the hallway in the direction opposite from where Cerasi had disappeared. The two guards exchanged glances.

"Daan!" the first guard hissed. "The girl was right! They're attacking!"

Qui-Gon was out the door, lightsaber in hand, before the guards could turn and react. Obi-Wan raced alongside him.

The guards fired their blasters rapidly as soon as they saw the Jedi. But they were too late. Obi-Wan and Qui-Gon deflected the fire with their lightsabers without missing a step.

Moving in synch, they jumped the last few meters to the guards, feet first. Deflecting blaster fire with their lightsabers, they hit the guards in the chest with a powerful kick. The guards flew back, their blasters flying out of their hands.

"Cover me," Qui-Gon instructed Obi-Wan crisply. He moved to the door. As he began to slice through the lock with his lightsaber, the guards recovered and reached for the electro-jabbers on their belts.

Obi-Wan didn't wait for them to rise. He leaped over them so that they would need to turn and twist to attack. He knocked the electro-jabber out of one guard's hand with a kick and sliced down with his lightsaber toward the other. The guard howled and dropped his weapon.

"Don't move," Obi-Wan warned them, keeping his lightsaber over their heads.

The lock gave, and Qui-Gon pushed open the door. He stopped, stricken at the heart by Tahl's appearance. She had gone through Temple training with him. She had always been beautiful, a tall woman from the planet Noori, with eyes striped gold and green and skin the color of dark honey.

Now she appeared thin and wasted. Her beautiful skin was marred by a white scar that ran from one eye and curved around her chin. The other eye was covered with a patch.

"Tahl," he said, keeping his voice steady. "It's Qui-Gon."

"Ah, rescue at last," she said in the gently mocking tone that had always made him smile. "Do I look that bad, old friend?"

He realized then that she could not see.

"You look as lovely as ever," he said. "But can you wait on the compliments? My hands are full at the moment."

"I'm afraid I'm a little weak," Tahl confessed.

"I'll carry you." Qui-Gon scooped up Tahl in his arms. She felt as light as a child. "Can you hang onto my neck?" he asked.

He felt her nod as her arms tightened around him. "Just get me out of here," she said. "I've had better food in a Hutt cantina."

Just then Qui-Gon heard the sound he'd hoped he wouldn't: rapid blaster fire. Reinforcements had arrived. Obi-Wan was in trouble. His time had run out.

He proceeded cautiously to the door. He peered out.

Six soldiers had charged out of their quarters and were shooting at Obi-Wan from the end of the hall. Obi-Wan had flung open a door and was using it for cover. The soldiers had rearmed the two on the ground, so there were now eight soldiers to fight.

"What's the bad news?" Tahl asked.

"Eight so far," Qui-Gon said. "Maybe more coming."

"Piece of cake for you," she said weakly.

"Just what I was about to say."

Blaster fire rebounded off the door that Obi-Wan crouched behind. The doors were armored,

Obi-Wan realized. They could use that to their advantage.

Qui-Gon flung his own door wide open and stepped out behind it, making a quick calculation. Obi-Wan had held off the soldiers so far by periodically deflecting blaster fire back at them with his lightsaber, but they would soon realize that he wasn't armed with a blaster.

Then they would rush him.

Qui-Gon looked over at Obi-Wan. It was time to take the offensive again. But he couldn't endanger Tahl, and she was too weak to walk. They were stuck. He would not leave Tahl. He didn't even want to put her down again. If he was separated from her, he might not be able to get to her again.

"Leave me, Qui-Gon," Tahl murmured to him. "I'll be no worse off than I was before. Do not let them capture you, too."

"Have a little faith, will you?" Qui-Gon countered gently.

Suddenly, blaster fire erupted from the opposite end of the hall. Now they were surrounded!

But after a moment Qui-Gon realized that the blaster fire was directed *at the soldiers.*

Or, he realized suddenly, at least it *sounded* like blaster fire. Cerasi hadn't left after creating a diversion, as she'd promised.

The soldiers dived around the corner for

cover. Qui-Gon glanced back down the other end just in time to see Cerasi fire another laser-ball. It hit the wall, and blaster fire echoed down the hall.

The guards now fired blindly, unwilling to risk exposure by coming around the corner. Obi-Wan stepped out. He was easily able to deflect the wild shots with his lightsaber. Holding Tahl against his chest with one arm, Qui-Gon raised his lightsaber to catch any blaster fire that Obi-Wan was unable to deflect. Together they moved backward down the hallway toward the storage room.

As they moved, Obi-Wan flung open door after door. They swung outward, helping to block blaster fire. The soldiers kept up a steady stream of fire, but Cerasi loaded and shot laser-balls just as fast, and the soldiers were convinced they were under attack.

Qui-Gon and Obi-Wan reached the safety of the storage room. Cerasi dashed forward.

"Hurry," she urged. "I'm running low."

She continued shooting as Obi-Wan slid back the grate and Qui-Gon climbed down one-handed, Tahl hugging his neck.

"Now!" Obi-Wan yelled.

Cerasi hurried down after Qui-Gon. Obi-Wan followed, setting the grate back in place.

"Thank you, Cerasi." Qui-Gon spoke quietly.

"We could not have done this without your bravery."

"Obi-Wan helped us this morning," Cerasi replied carelessly, as if risking her life were nothing. "I just returned the favor."

"Why did you think of claiming to be Wehutti's daughter?" Obi-Wan asked her as she led the way back.

"Because I am," Cerasi answered.

"But you said your father was dead," Obi-Wan pointed out.

"He is dead to me," Cerasi replied with a shrug. "But occasionally he comes in handy. Just like most Elders."

She looked over her shoulder at Obi-Wan and flashed him a grin. Obi-Wan's eyes shone back.

Qui-Gon saw in the moment of their exchange that something had deepened between them. They were intimates now, communicating without words. The adventure they had shared that morning had united them.

Qui-Gon felt his earlier anger drain away. He supposed that Obi-Wan had a lonely existence at times, traveling with someone older than himself. He must miss being with boys and girls his own age. It was good that he could bond so strongly with another.

Why should it make Qui-Gon so uneasy?

CHAPTER 12

Qui-Gon settled Tahl into a nest of quilts and blankets, the best the Young had to offer. He stood over her for a moment. She had tired from the short battle and she fell asleep almost immediately. He could feel the flicker of her living Force, but it was only a flicker. Tahl's memory of how she got her injuries was gone. She remembered being caught in the middle of a battle, but she could not remember being wounded or blinded.

Qui-Gon sat back against the wall to think. Their mission was over. They had only to wait until the fighting died down. Cerasi had assured him that she could get the Jedi out of the city without endangering Tahl. He would bring Tahl back to Coruscant and hope that the Jedi healing arts would bring her back to the vibrant strength he remembered so well.

Qui-Gon knew he would leave behind a world

in chaos. Children battling to save it. Elders locked in conflict, willing to sacrifice the population for their cause.

Yet he must leave. His first duty was to get Tahl back. Then he would ask Yoda's permission to return. The Jedi Master would not grant it, most likely. The Jedi did not go to worlds and meddle in their affairs unless they were requested to do so. Only in extraordinary circumstances would they interfere, or if a world was threatening the peace and security of others. The inhabitants of Melida/Daan were locked in its conflict, hurting no other world but their own.

Obi-Wan had asked permission to go above ground with Cerasi. Qui-Gon had granted it. He knew that when he told Obi-Wan that they must leave, his Padawan would not want to go. Yet Obi-Wan would obey him. It was his first duty as a Padawan, and Obi-Wan was a Jedi to the bone.

Their mission was close to success. Yet foreboding lodged in Qui-Gon's chest like a heavy stone. His instinct was warning him, but he could not place what the warning was, or how it would affect him.

He heard running footsteps, and Nield burst into the room with Obi-Wan and Cerasi. Qui-Gon was struck with how the three moved in the same rhythm, their strides matching perfectly despite Obi-Wan's long legs and Cerasi's more slender build.

"Gather around, everyone!" Nield cried. "We have news!"

Nield leaped up on top of the grandest tomb. Boys and girls swarmed around him, coming from the strategy stations around the room and from the adjoining tunnels. They turned expectant faces up to him.

"Our battle is over," Nield said. "We have achieved total victory!"

The Young cheered wildly. Nield held up a hand.

"Our raid on the weapons storehouse of the Daan was a success. We have stolen the weapons the Daan did not waste in attacking the Melida or shooting at imaginary attackers. We have deposited them in the North Tunnel. The Melida" Nield paused, grinned, "— blew up their own storehouses so that the Daan would not get their weapons!"

The Young let out wild hoots of laughter. They shouted with joy.

"We have delivered our messages to both sides, letting them know that the Young were behind the battles, and that we have succeeded in stealing their arms. Without weapons, the

Elders cannot fight each other. Today we have taken a giant step toward peace!"

Exhilaration raced through the room like a current. Qui-Gon watched as Nield leaned down and grabbed Cerasi's hand. He pulled her up to stand next to him. Then he reached down for Obi-Wan. Smiling, Obi-Wan leaped up on the tomb to take his place beside the two leaders.

The Young reached up to touch his tunic. Obi-Wan reached down to touch their hands and accept their congratulations. He linked arms with Cerasi and Nield. Never once did he glance at Qui-Gon. It was as though the Jedi Knight wasn't in the room. It was as though Obi-Wan was not a Jedi.

It was as though he was part of them. As though he had become one of the Young.

CHAPTER 13

Qui-Gon left the main room and found a quiet place in an adjoining tunnel to contact Yoda. The Jedi Master appeared in miniature hologram form. Quickly, Qui-Gon filled him in on the situation and the rescue of Tahl.

Yoda passed a hand over his forehead in distress. "Relieved I am to hear this news," he said. "Concerned I am to hear that Tahl is ailing. Needs care, she does."

"I will leave as soon as she's stronger and it is safe," Qui-Gon promised. "But I leave a situation here on Melida/Daan that is volatile."

Yoda nodded several times. "Heard you, I have, Qui-Gon. But remind you I must that neither the Melida or the Daan have asked for our help. Almost sacrificed one Jedi, I did. Willing sacrifice two more, I am not."

"We could bring Tahl back and then return," Qui-Gon pointed out.

Yoda paused. "Before the Jedi Council you must go," he said finally. "Make this decision alone I cannot. Cared for, Tahl must be. Then decide we will, if help we must give. Until then, taking sides the Jedi must not do. Jeopardize peace it would. Avoid you must, angering one side or another."

As usual, Yoda had a point. Already the Melida would be angry when they heard that the Jedi had broken into their barracks. And if word got out that Obi-Wan had gone on the raid into Daan territory, that would anger the Daan.

He bowed. "I hope to find Tahl ready tomorrow. I will return soon, Master."

"Look forward to that day, I will," Yoda said gently. The hologram flickered and disappeared.

"Go back? We can't go back!" Obi-Wan exclaimed. "We can't leave the Young now. They need us."

"We have received no official request to stabilize the planet," Qui-Gon said patiently. "Perhaps back on Coruscant, the Jedi Council will —"

"We can't wait for the Council to review this," Obi-Wan interrupted, shaking his head. "If we wait too long, the Melida and the Daan will rearm. The time to act is now."

"Obi-Wan, listen to me," Qui-Gon said sternly.

"Yoda has directed us to come back. Tahl needs care."

"She needs rest and med care," Obi-Wan argued. "We can get that for her here. Cerasi can tell me where to go. We can bring a medic back here, or find a place to keep her that would be safe —"

"No," Qui-Gon said, shaking his head. "She must be brought back to the Temple. We can do no more here, Padawan. We will leave tomorrow."

"Part of our mission was to try to stabilize the planet, if we could," Obi-Wan insisted. "We haven't done that. But we *can* if we stay!"

"We have not been asked —"

" We have been asked, by the Young!" Obi-Wan exclaimed.

"That is not an official request," Qui-Gon replied testily. The boy was beginning to try his patience.

"You have broken the rules before, Qui-Gon," Obi-Wan argued. "Back on Gala, you left me to travel to the hill country when you were instructed to stay at the palace. You break the rules when it suits you to do so."

Qui-Gon took a deep breath, trying to control his temper. He would not match Obi-Wan's anger with his own. "I break the rules not because it suits me, but because sometimes dur-

ing a mission the rules get in the way," he s
carefully. "That is not the case here. I believe
Yoda is right."

"But —" Obi-Wan interrupted, but Qui-Gon
held up a hand.

"Tomorrow we will leave, Padawan," he said
firmly.

Suddenly, a roar rose from the Young, who
were gathered in the far corner of the vault.
Cerasi ran over to the Jedi, her face beaming.

"It is official!" she cried. "In the absence of a
response to our request for peace, we have is-
sued a declaration of war on the Elders. If they
do not agree immediately to Melida/Daan peace
negotiations, we will attack them with their own
weapons. They must respond to us now." She
turned shining eyes to Obi-Wan. "This is the
last push we must do to change the history of
Melida/Daan. We need your help more than
ever!"

CHAPTER 14

Choked with anger and frustration, Obi-Wan could not answer Cerasi.

It was Qui-Gon who said gently, "I'm sorry, Cerasi. We must leave tomorrow."

Obi-Wan didn't wait to see Cerasi's reaction. He could only turn away, sick at heart. He had let her down.

It was no use. He couldn't change Qui-Gon's mind. Silently, Obi-Wan helped him minister to Tahl. They prepared and fed her broth and tea. Cerasi had brought Qui-Gon a medpac, and he was able to treat some of Tahl's wounds. Already, she seemed stronger. She would be ready to travel by tomorrow, Obi-Wan knew. The Jedi powers of recuperation were remarkable.

As soon as Tahl was settled, Obi-Wan sat against the wall and tried to calm his raging heart. Something was happening to him that he didn't understand. He felt as though there were two parts of him: a Jedi, and a person called Obi-Wan. Always before, he could not separate being a Jedi from being himself.

He had not been a Jedi with Nield and Cerasi. He had been one of them. He had not needed the Force to feel connected to something larger than himself.

Now Qui-Gon was asking him to leave his friends just as they needed him. He had pledged to help them, had battled alongside them, and now he had to go, just because an elder told him so.

Loyalty had seemed such an easy concept back at the Temple. He had thought that he would be the best Padawan it was possible to be. He would meld his mind and body with his Master, and serve.

But he did not want to serve like this. Obi-Wan closed his eyes as his frustration again boiled up inside him. He pressed his hands between his knees to calm their shaking. He felt frightened at what was happening to him. He couldn't go to Qui-Gon for counsel. He didn't believe in his Master's counsel any longer. Yet neither could he oppose it.

Across the room, Nield was just as agitated, prowling around the headquarters silently. Everyone was waiting for the Melida and Daan councils to respond to the declaration of war. The long evening shaded into night, and still no word came.

"They did not take us seriously," Nield said bitterly. "We must strike again, and strike hard enough to make them sit up and take notice."

Cerasi put her hand on his arm. "But not tonight. Everyone needs rest. Tomorrow we can plan."

Nield nodded. Cerasi lowered the glow rods until they were only faint spots of illumination against the dark walls, like distant stars in a black sky.

Qui-Gon rolled himself up in his cloak and went to sleep by Tahl's side in case she called for him in the night. Obi-Wan watched as the boys and girls around him settled into exhausted sleep. Over in the corner, he saw Cerasi and Nield huddled together, talking quietly.

I should be with them, Obi-Wan thought bitterly. He belonged with them, talking about strategy and plans. Instead he had to sit silently, passively, watching their dedication, their fire. Cerasi hadn't looked at him once during the long evening. Nield hadn't either. They were no doubt disappointed and angry.

Hesitantly, Obi-Wan rose. Even if he left them tomorrow, they had to know that he had no choice. He walked softly among the sleeping children and approached them.

"I wanted to say good-bye now," he said. "We'll be leaving early tomorrow." He paused. "I'm sorry I can't stay to help you. I want to."

"We understand," Nield said in a clipped tone. "You must obey your elder."

"It's not obedience as much as respect," Obi-Wan explained. His words sounded lame, even to him.

"Ah," Cerasi said, nodding. "My trouble is, I never got this respect thing. My father told me what was right, and he was always wrong. What does it matter, he'd say, if thousands die, or millions die? The sky is still blue overhead, and our world still remains. The cause is what's important. And so your Jedi boss tells you what you must do, and you do it. Even though you know he's wrong. And that is called respect." She looked at Nield. "Maybe I've been living in the dark too long. But I just can't see that."

Obi-Wan stood awkwardly in front of them. He felt confused. The Jedi way had always shimmered clear as a fountain of pure water to him. But Cerasi had muddied the water, clouded it with doubt.

"I would help if I could," he said finally. "If there was something I knew I could do that would make a difference —"

Nield and Cerasi looked at each other, then back at him.

"What is it?" Obi-Wan asked.

"We do have a plan," Cerasi said.

Obi-Wan crouched down next to them. "Tell me."

Nield and Cerasi leaned closer, their foreheads almost touching Obi-Wan's.

"You know that there are deflection towers ringing the perimeter of the city," Cerasi whispered. "There are also towers around the Melida center. These towers control the particle shields, preventing entry, and separating Melida from Daan."

"Yes, I've seen them," Obi-Wan said, nodding.

Nield leaned forward. "We've been in contact with the Young outside the city," he said. "I've sent a message to them telling them that we have succeeded in capturing the weapons of both Melida and Daan. There are several destroyed villages ringing the city. Many of the children live there, or in the countryside. Hundreds. Thousands, if we take in a wider area. They are all connected by a network. If we can destroy the particle shields, they will march on Zehava."

"And they have weapons, too," Cerasi added quietly. "We would have an army. Not only would the Elders be outnumbered, they would have nothing to fight with. We could win a war without one death — if we are careful, and the Elders are smart enough to surrender."

"It sounds like a good plan," Obi-Wan said. "But how are you going to knock out the deflection towers?"

"That's our problem," Nield said. "They can only be destroyed from the air. All we need is an air transport."

"We can't use floaters," Cerasi explained. "The deflection towers have defense systems. Floaters wouldn't be fast enough or agile enough. We need a starfighter."

Cerasi and Nield held Obi-Wan's gaze.

"We know you flew some sort of fast transport into Melida/Daan. Will you fly us on the mission?" Cerasi asked.

Obi-Wan's breath left him. Cerasi and Nield were asking a great deal. This would go beyond a Padawan's disobedience. It would defy Yoda himself.

Qui-Gon would be within his rights to send him back to the Temple. He would probably have to appear before the Jedi Council. And Qui-Gon would have the right to dismiss him as his Padawan.

"We can leave at dawn," Nield said. "The mission should only take an hour, maybe a little more. Then you can take Tahl back to Coruscant."

"The destruction of the particle shield will actually make it easier for you to smuggle Tahl out of Zehava," Cerasi pointed out.

"But if the starfighter is damaged, it could mean she can't leave at all," Obi-Wan said. "It would doom our mission to failure, and perhaps make me responsible for Tahl's death."

Cerasi bit her lip. "It was wrong of me to mock you before," she said awkwardly, as if she were unused to apologies. "I know the Jedi code guides the way you live. And we know we are asking too much from you. If we weren't desperate, we wouldn't do it. You've done so much already for us."

"As you have done for us," Obi-Wan said. "We could not have rescued Tahl without you."

"It is our only chance for peace," Nield said. "Once the Elders see our numbers, they will have no choice but surrender."

Obi-Wan glanced over at Qui-Gon's sleeping form. He owed his Master so much. Qui-Gon had fought alongside him, even saved his life. They had a bond.

Yet he had a bond with Nield and Cerasi, too. The shortness of the time he'd known them made no difference. The current that ran between them was like nothing he'd ever experienced. And even though Cerasi apologized for mocking him, hadn't there been a germ of truth in her words? Was it right to obey when his heart told him it was wrong?

Cerasi's usual fierce green gaze had softened with compassion as she watched the struggle on his face. Nield met his gaze steadily, warmly. He, too, knew what they were asking Obi-Wan was a great sacrifice.

He would have to betray Qui-Gon, betray his life as a Jedi. For them. For their cause. They could ask this because they knew they were right.

Obi-Wan knew they were right, too. And he couldn't let them down. He could not make this decision as a Jedi. He would make it as a friend.

He took a deep breath. "I'll do it."

CHAPTER 15

They sneaked out before dawn. Cerasi led them to the Outer Circle through the tunnels. Then they left Zehava the same way Obi-Wan and Qui-Gon had arrived — through the Hall of Evidence, back to the trap. This time, Nield had brought finely spun carbon rope, which he tossed up to the surface. A strong magnet adhered to the metal slide, and they were able to scale it easily.

The hike to the transport went quickly in the cool gray light. The three of them had stuffed proton grenades in their packs. They were heavy, but they hardly felt the weight. They were anxious to get to the transport and start their mission.

When they reached the starfighter, Nield and Cerasi helped Obi-Wan uncover it from the branches and brush he and Qui-Gon had dragged over it. Nield beamed when he saw the sleek, small starfighter. Then he noticed the gash in the side panel. He turned to Obi-Wan.

"I guess I should have asked you something. Are you a good pilot?"

Obi-Wan looked at him blankly for a moment. Then Cerasi burst out laughing. Nield and Obi-Wan joined her, the sound bouncing off the canyon walls.

"I guess we'll find out," Cerasi said cheerfully.

They climbed into the starfighter. Obi-Wan slid into the pilot's seat. For a moment, he hesitated, staring at the controls. The last time he'd sat here, he'd landed the craft with Qui-Gon in the copilot's seat. Qui-Gon had kidded him about denting the side of the starfighter. Obi-Wan felt a pang of remorse. Was he doing the right thing? Was this cause worth betraying Qui-Gon?

Cerasi touched his wrist gently. "We know this is hard for you, Obi-Wan. That's what makes your sacrifice even more valuable to us."

"And we give you our deepest thanks," Nield said quietly.

Obi-Wan turned and met their eyes. He felt a shock, as though he were looking at himself. In the steady gazes of his friends he saw what was held in his own heart — the same dedication, the same fierceness, the same daring. He felt his confidence surge. He *was* doing the right thing. Maybe Qui-Gon would come to understand that.

He started the ion engines. "Let's get going."

"We should hit the perimeter towers first, then the center towers," Cerasi said. "We're going to have to do everything by sight. I don't have any coordinates for the nav computer."

"It won't be a problem," Obi-Wan said. He kept the engines at low power as the ship rose in order to clear the overhanging cliff. Then he pushed the engines to full power to soar above the canyon. No one told him to slow down.

"I'm going to have to do some defensive flying, so it's better if you two do the aiming," Obi-Wan said. "The station for the laser cannon is right in front of you, Cerasi."

Nield went to his own laser cannon station.

"I'll open up the emergency weapon sighting plate as we get closer," Obi-Wan said. "Remember to keep your eyes out for speeders. We're going to have to come in low to blast the deflection controls."

The two deflection towers flanking the main gate came into sight in seconds. "Here we go," Obi-Wan said, gritting his teeth.

"Floater on the right approaching," Cerasi

rapped out. "We must have turned up on scanners."

Obi-Wan cut sharply to the left, then veered right again. Surprised to see a starfighter heading straight for it, the floater turned sharply downward, firing at the same time. Obi-Wan made a minute adjustment that caused the ship to turn and the missile to harmlessly fall to his left. It crashed outside the city walls, causing an explosion.

"They won't do that very often," Cerasi noted. "They could level a building once we get over the city."

"They'll probably use smaller firepower," Nield agreed.

"We have to do this without blasting them out of the sky," Cerasi said worriedly. "We have to show them that our ultimate goal is peace."

"That's my job," Obi-Wan said. "The tower is in range. Let's blast it."

Another floater approached from the left, and he could see others taking to the air like a flock of insects, probably from the Daan military headquarters in the distance. Obi-Wan calculated the slower speed of the floaters. He had to stay level long enough for Cerasi and Nield to aim. He should have just enough time . . .

He opened the firing panel for Nield. Bracing

himself against the hull of the starfighter, Nield aimed his laser cannon. Cerasi waited, her fingers on her own control stick.

"Now!" Obi-Wan shouted, zooming closer to the deflection tower.

Cerasi and Nield fired the cannons. As soon as the projectiles were away, Obi-Wan pushed the engines to full power and climbed above the floater heading for his left flank. Blaster fire followed him. He took a small hit on his wing, but not enough to damage the craft.

Both Cerasi and Nield scored a direct hit on the tower. Obi-Wan felt the vibration of the blast ripple against the starfighter's hull. The floater rocked as it rode the wind vibrations, the driver struggling to retain control. The particle shield was briefly visible, then fractured in a shower of blue-tinged energy atoms.

Obi-Wan, Cerasi, and Nield cheered, even as Obi-Wan circled around to hit the next tower. Now the military floaters were almost on him.

"Seven floaters," Cerasi said, counting. Her face creased in worry. "Can we do this, Obi-Wan?"

"If we do it fast. Can you aim upside down?" Obi-Wan asked, hovering out of the floater's range.

Cerasi grinned. "No problem."

Nield positioned his laser cannon. "Do it."

Obi-Wan pushed the engines. The starfighter rocketed down through the sky at full speed. He knew that technically he was going too fast for this altitude, but he also knew he could handle the craft. And there was no one in the copilot's seat to remind him of star aviation rules, or warn him of the dangers. Exhilaration raced through him. For the first time in his life, he had no one to answer to. There were no Jedi rules or superior wisdom aboard this ship.

He zigzagged on the descent, pushing the ship as much as he dared. The floaters hung back and fired, afraid of colliding with the starship. Using the Force as a guide, Obi-Wan was able to avoid the worst fire.

As he got closer, the speeders grew more daring. One came at him dead-on, firing as it went.

"Ready —" Obi-Wan shouted.

At the last moment, he flipped the starfighter over and dived under the floater, maneuvering the craft so that it had a clear shot at the tower.

Nield and Cerasi fired. The deflection tower blew, scattering metal and parts. Obi-Wan flipped the starfighter right-side up and climbed at top speed. The floaters frantically dived to avoid getting hit.

"Everyone okay?" Obi-Wan asked.

"Dizzy, but okay," Cerasi said, wiping sweat off her forehead. "That was incredible flying."

"Okay, follow the wall," Nield directed. "We'll hit the towers one by one around the perimeter."

The military floaters pursued them, but they could not fly as high or go as fast as a starfighter. More floaters joined the chase as they flew. To hit each deflection tower, Obi-Wan had to practice the same too-fast maneuvering to avoid being blasted by the speeders or colliding with them. Their advantage was the speed and agility of the starfighter and the incredible accuracy of Cerasi and Nield.

One by one, they destroyed each tower, the speeders hard on their flank. The speeders tried to capture Obi-Wan in a pincer movement, but he was too quick for them.

When they saw the last tower go up, the three let out a whoop of exultation. Cerasi leaned over and hugged Obi-Wan. Nield pounded him on the back.

"I knew we could count on you, friend," he said joyfully. He checked his laser cannon. "We have plenty of firepower left. What do you say we blow the Halls of Evidence into nanospecs?"

Cerasi frowned. "Now? But Nield, we need to get back. We have to hit both Melida and Daan for peace negotiations while they're weak."

"And besides, there could be people inside," Obi-Wan pointed out.

Cerasi looked at Nield. "We said we would do this without taking a life."

Nield bit his lip as he glanced out the spaceport down to the surface of Zehava. "The sooner those halls of hate are blown up, the sooner everyone on this planet can breathe again," he murmured. "I despise everything they stand for."

"I know," Cerasi said. "So do I. But let's take one step at a time."

"All right," Nield agreed reluctantly. "But let's do one last thing. Before we land, let's do a quick loop over the countryside. Deila was waiting to pass the message that the perimeter shields had been blown. The Scavenger Young should be mobilizing."

Obi-Wan flew in widening circles over the countryside. Everywhere they saw young people, boys and girls, streaming out from farms and villages and woods. They were already beginning to clog the road into Zehava. Some rode on battered landspeeders or souped-up turbo-tractors. Those who walked formed columns, marching in military style. When they saw the starfighter overhead, they waved and shouted greetings the three could not hear. Obi-Wan dipped his wings in a return salute.

Tears stood in Cerasi's eyes. "I will never forget this day," she said. "And I will never forget what you did for us, Obi-Wan Kenobi."

Obi-Wan turned the starfighter back toward the landing area. He didn't care how angry Qui-Gon was, or if he got sent back to the Temple. This moment was worth it.

CHAPTER 16

Qui-Gon had woken early and checked on Tahl. She was sleeping deeply. That was good. Sleep was the best healer until he could get her to Coruscant.

He saw that Obi-Wan had disappeared, along with Nield and Cerasi. No doubt he wanted a last outing with his friends before he left. Qui-Gon would let it pass. He knew it was hard for the boy to leave them.

And he had a plan of his own.

He had asked a quiet girl named Roenni to watch over Tahl. Then he'd traveled through the tunnels to the route he had mapped out last night, slipping away while the rest of the Young were celebrating their victory.

When he emerged above ground in the abandoned neighborhood at the border of Melida and Daan territory, it was still dark. A few stars still twinkled in a navy sky that shaded to gray at the horizon.

Qui-Gon had waited in the alley until he was sure all the people he'd invited had arrived. Then he walked to the partially bombed out building on the corner.

Last night he'd sent a note to Wehutti by one of the Young messengers. He had asked for a meeting between the Melida Council and the Daan Council. He had suggested that it was in their best interest to attend. He had news of the Young that they must know.

Until now, he hadn't been sure if anyone would show up. He still wasn't sure if one side or the other would try to capture him. It was a desperate gamble. He was prepared for anything. But he had to make a last try for peace before he left Melida/Daan. He had seen the heartbreak on Obi-Wan's face. He would do it for his Padawan.

Near a broken window, he paused to listen for a moment.

"And where is the Jedi?" a voice asked coldly. "If this is another dirty Melida trick, I swear by the honored memory of our martyrs that we will retaliate."

"A dirty *Daan* trick, more likely." Qui-Gon recognized Wehutti's voice. "For it's a coward's trick, worthy of your worthless ancestors, to lure your enemy to a meeting under false pretenses. Our troops can be here in seconds."

"And what will they do? Throw pebbles?" The other voice was amused. "Didn't the Melida blow up their own weapons stores, fearing the attacking Daan?"

"And didn't the Daan allow their own stores to be stolen right under their noses?" Wehutti snapped.

Qui-Gon knew it was time for him to enter. He climbed over a half-demolished wall. The Melida council members stood on one side of the room, heavily armed and dressed in plastoid armor. The Daan stood on the opposite side, almost identically dressed and armed. Each member of each group bore scars and signs of healed wounds. Several were missing limbs, or breathed through breath masks. It was hard to tell the two ravaged groups apart.

"No tricks, no stratagems," Qui-Gon said, striding to the middle of the room. "And if Melida and Daan will cooperate, I won't take up too much time, either."

The Daan council members looked as skeptical as the Melida, Qui-Gon thought as he surveyed the room. At least the two groups had something in common: distrust.

"What news of the Young have you brought us?" Wehutti asked impatiently.

"And why should we care what children do?" an elder Daan asked contemptuously.

"Because yesterday they made you look like fools," Qui-Gon answered mildly. He waited out the indrawn breaths and looks of avid hatred directed his way. "And, on a more practical note, they have stolen most of your weapons," he added. "They have asked for disarmament, and you have ignored them. Obviously, they are quite capable of getting what they want."

"All we have to do is walk in and take back our weapons," the Daan leader said, rasping through a breath mask. "Candy from a baby."

"I warn you," Qui-Gon said, turning to catch the eye of everyone in the room. "Do not underestimate the Young. They have learned how to fight from you. They have learned determination from you. And they have their own ideas."

"Is this what you brought us here to hear?" the Daan leader growled. "If so, I have heard enough."

"For once, I agree with Gueni," Wehutti said, referring to the Daan in the breath mask. "This is a waste of time."

"I must urge you to reconsider," Qui-Gon said. "If you form a coalition government, you might be able to take control of Zehava, and thus of Melida/Daan. If not, the Young will win this war. They will end up ruling their elders. And though their aims are pure, I fear for the cost that will bring."

Wehutti started from the room, followed by the Melida leaders. "Join with the Daan? You're dreaming!"

Quickly, Gueni followed suit, as though he did not want the Melida to be the first to leave. The other Daan followed on his heels. "Unthinkable!"

Suddenly, the sound of an explosion caused the remaining windows to vibrate. The Daan and Melida looked at each other.

"This is a trick!" Wehutti roared. "The foul Daan are attacking us!"

"The detestable Melida are attacking!" Gueni cried at the same time. "Fiends!"

Qui-Gon strode to the window. He looked out, but could see nothing. As he scanned the area, another explosion ripped through the silence. It had come from the Daan sector, he calculated. But what could it have been?

In the next second, Gueni's comlink began to beep. The Elder Daan hurried to a corner to take the message in private. While Gueni listened, his back to the room, Qui-Gon began to worry. Obi-Wan had disappeared that morning. He hoped his Padawan wasn't involved in whatever was going on. Using the Force, he tried to establish a connection with Obi-Wan. But he could feel nothing. No distress, no confusion, no assurance. Only . . . a void.

When Gueni turned back to the group, he looked shaken. "Reports have come in that two deflection towers have been blown in the Daan sector."

One of the Daan warriors went for his weapon. "I knew it! The filthy Melida—"

"No!" Gueni cried hoarsely. "It was the Young."

Slowly, the Daan's hand fell to his side. The Melida who had begun to reach for his weapon stopped as well. A babble of conversation rose.

"Those children could not do it on their own! The deplorable Melida are behind this!" one of the Daan council members shouted.

"The lying Daan are always quick to accuse without facts!" a Melida roared back.

Qui-Gon leaned against the sill and waited out the argument. Sometimes, it was better to sit back and wait for events to unfold.

Comlinks began to beep. Melida and Daan alike spoke into them, their faces registering shock. Reports flooded in from both sides. One by one, the deflection towers went down. First on the perimeter, then in the center. The explosions got closer as the last towers were blown.

"The Young are pouring in from the countryside," Gueni reported, a look of amazement on his face. "The city is now open. Defenseless. And they are armed."

Melida and Daan faced each other. Now they knew the threat that faced them was serious.

"Do you see now that you must join together?" Qui-Gon asked quietly. "The Young only want peace. You can give it to them. Don't you want to rebuild your city?"

"They say they want peace, but they wage war," Wehutti said contemptuously. "Well, we can give them a war to make our ancestors proud. We may have lost some weapons, but we are not defenseless."

"And we have weapons remaining as well," a Daan said quickly. "Shipments are arriving this very afternoon from our stores outside the city."

"They will collapse at any sign of resistance," a Melida woman chimed in. "We can fight them."

"But not together," Wehutti said. "The glorious Melida can defeat them without Daan help."

"For once, do not overestimate yourselves!" Qui-Gon spoke sharply. "You don't have weapons. You don't have air support. You have an army made of Elders and the wounded. Think of what you're saying. There are thousands of them!"

Both sides of the room grew silent. Wehutti and Gueni exchanged a glance. Qui-Gon glimpsed surrender underneath the sizzling distrust.

"Perhaps the Jedi is right," Gueni said reluctantly. "I see only one way to defeat them. We must join our armies and weapons. But the Jedi must lead us."

Wehutti nodded slowly. "It's the only way we can be sure that the Daan will not turn on us once the battle is won."

"It is our only assurance also," Gueni said. "We cannot trust the word of the Melida."

Qui-Gon shook his head. "I did not come here to lead you into battle. I came here to urge you to find a way toward peace."

"But there is no peace!" Wehutti cried. "The Young have drawn the battle lines!"

"These are your children!" Qui-Gon cried out. He had lost his patience in the face of the cruel obstinacy of both sides. He controlled his voice and went on. "I, for one, will not kill children. Why are you so willing to do so?" He turned to Wehutti. "What about Cerasi? Are you willing to march into battle against your own daughter?"

Wehutti paled. His clenched fist uncurled.

"My grandson Rica is underground," Gueni said.

"I have not seen my Deila in two years," a woman Melida said quietly.

Other Daan and Melida looked uncertain. There was a long pause.

"All right," Wehutti said at last. "If you will be our emissary, we will open talks with the Young."

Gueni nodded. "The Daan agree. You are right, Qui-Gon. We cannot wage war against our children."

CHAPTER 17

"We will not meet with them," Nield told Qui-Gon furiously. "I know what their promises are worth. They agree to meet as a diversion. They will tell us we must disarm. And then the fighting will begin again. This surrender is too soon. If we relent, they'll think we're weak."

"They know you have backed them into a corner," Qui-Gon argued. "They're willing to talk. You succeeded, Nield. Now take your victory."

Cerasi crossed her arms. "We did not succeed by being fools, Qui-Gon."

Qui-Gon turned away with a sigh. He had been arguing with Cerasi and Nield since he'd returned. It had done no good. It was out of his hands, anyway.

Obi-Wan sat at the makeshift table, watching. He hadn't offered an opinion, or tried to sway Cerasi or Nield. Qui-Gon had noted this with surprise. Obi-Wan had wanted peace on this planet. Why did he stand back now? Once again, when Qui-Gon tried to connect with his Padawan, he found a void.

Headquarters was now crowded with the boys and girls who had arrived from the country. More congregated aboveground, gathered in parks and squares. The Young had mobilized, bringing whatever food they had and instituting a supply line. It would take all day to get everyone fed, but they were determined to succeed.

"How did you blow the deflection towers?" Qui-Gon asked Nield and Cerasi curiously. It was a question that had been bothering him since he'd heard the news. "You'd have to hit them from the air. But floaters couldn't do that job. You'd need . . ."

Qui-Gon paused. He turned to face Obi-Wan. Slowly, Obi-Wan pushed his chair back. Qui-Gon heard it scrape against the stone floor. Then he stood. He did not fidget or look away. He met Qui-Gon's gaze.

"So it was you," Qui-Gon said. "You took the starfighter. You took it knowing it was our only way off the planet. You took it knowing it was the only hope for Tahl."

Obi-Wan nodded.

Cerasi and Nield glanced from one Jedi to the other. Cerasi began to speak, but thought better of it. The tension between Qui-Gon and Obi-Wan was private.

"Please come with me, Obi-Wan," Qui-Gon said curtly.

He led the way to an adjacent tunnel where they could talk privately. He waited a few moments to compose himself. Bitterness had no place here. Yet he felt it surge within him. Obi-Wan had broken his trust.

He did not know what to say. His emotions swamped him. Qui-Gon recalled his Temple training with an effort. He would admonish his Padawan according to Jedi rules. First, he would describe the offense. It was the duty of the Master to do so without judgment.

Grateful for a guide, Qui-Gon took a deep breath. "You were instructed not to take sides."

"Yes," Obi-Wan responded calmly. It was the duty of a Padawan to agree to his fault without argument.

"You were instructed to be available to leave at any time," he said.

"Yes," Obi-Wan replied.

"You were instructed that Tahl's health was your first concern. Yet you endangered that health by taking our only form of transport on a dangerous mission."

"Yes," Obi-Wan agreed.

Qui-Gon swallowed painfully. "By doing all this, you not only put Tahl at risk, but the peace process on Melida/Daan as well."

Obi-Wan hesitated for the first time. "I aided the peace process —"

"That is your interpretation," Qui-Gon interrupted. "It was not your instruction. Your Master and Jedi Master Yoda had decided that Jedi intervention at this stage could only prejudice either the Melida or Daan, thereby sabotaging the peace process. You were told this. Is that true, Obi-Wan?"

"Yes," Obi-Wan admitted. "It is true."

Qui-Gon paused. He gathered himself to deliver the Jedi wisdom of the Master and Padawan relationship. How the rules had evolved over thousands of years. How the Padawan's pledge of obedience had nothing to do with power, but everything to do with the gaining of wisdom and the humility of service. How he was not here to punish Obi-Wan, or even to teach him, but to aid Obi-Wan's own journey and enlightenment until the day he grew to become a Jedi Knight.

"I don't care," Obi-Wan said, breaking into his thoughts.

"You don't care about what?" Qui-Gon asked, startled. Usually, a Padawan was silent after his admission, waiting for the Master to decide on their next step.

"I don't care that I broke the rules," Obi-Wan said. "It was right to break them."

Qui-Gon took a breath. "And was it right to break my trust?"

Obi-Wan nodded. "I'm sorry I had to. But yes."

Qui-Gon felt Obi-Wan's words enter him like a blade. He saw in a flash that since he had taken Obi-Wan as his apprentice, he had been waiting for this moment. Waiting for the betrayal. The strike. He had hardened his heart, preparing himself for it.

And yet he was not prepared at all.

"Qui-Gon, you must understand," Obi-Wan said quietly. "I've found something here. All my life, I have been told what is right, what is best. The path has been pointed out to me. That was a great gift, and I'm grateful for all I've learned. But here on this world all those abstractions I've learned suddenly fit into something concrete. Something I can see. Something real." Obi-Wan gestured back toward the headquarters of the Young. "These people feel like my people. This cause feels like my cause. It calls to me like nothing I've ever felt before."

Qui-Gon's astonishment turned to grief and anger at himself. Obi-Wan had been swept away. He should have stepped in earlier. He should have remembered that Obi-Wan was just a boy.

He chose his words with care. "The situation here is heartbreaking, yes. It is a hard one to walk away from. That's why I tried to resolve it before we left. But walk away we must, Padawan."

Obi-Wan's face turned stony.

"Obi-Wan," Qui-Gon said gently. "Everything you think you found here you already have. You are a Jedi. What you need is distance and a little time for reflection."

"I don't need to reflect," Obi-Wan said stiffly.

"That is your choice," Qui-Gon said. "But still, you must accompany me back to the Temple. I need to gather some things for Tahl in the city. When I return, I expect to find you packed and ready to go."

He started back to the main tunnel. Obi-Wan did not move.

"Come, Padawan," he said.

Reluctantly, Obi-Wan trailed behind him. Qui-Gon felt worry fill him. There was something closed in Obi-Wan, something unmoveable, that he had never sensed in his apprentice before. It would be good to return to the Temple, where the wisdom of Yoda and the calm surroundings could help Obi-Wan find his center again.

Qui-Gon heard a roar from the main tunnel, voices shouting, pounding feet on stone. He quickened his pace and burst into the space, Obi-Wan at his heels.

Nield spun around to face them. "The offer for negotiation was a trick. The Elders have attacked!"

CHAPTER 18

Chaos reigned in the tunnels. The passage-ways were choked with bodies, children desperately trying to escape the battle raging above. Some were wounded. Others hurriedly tried to arm themselves for the counterattack. Hundreds of the Young were trapped above in open parks and squares. They needed reinforcements.

"We need medics and a supply line for weapons," Cerasi said.

"We need to strike back hard!" Nield cried.

Obi-Wan rushed to huddle with Cerasi and Nield. Qui-Gon saw anguish on all three faces. It was right that his Padawan help while he could.

But they had to get Tahl off-planet immediately. Now it was imperative.

Qui-Gon hurried to her side. She was sitting up, listening intently to what was going on around her.

He crouched by her side. "I had hoped to go back to the city to find more med supplies and borrow a floater, but I'm afraid that's impossible now. War has broken out, and we must leave immediately."

She nodded. "It's all right. I can walk, Qui-Gon. Your medicine has already helped me. I can make it, if you guide me."

Qui-Gon bent to gather up their things. They had lost their survival packs, but he had gathered supplies over the past few days. He stashed them in a pack Cerasi had given him.

When he turned to search for Obi-Wan, the boy was gone.

Cerasi and Nield were gone as well. Qui-Gon dropped the pack and searched the adjoining tunnels. He went as far as he could, but he was wasting time. Obi-Wan had probably gone to the surface with Cerasi and Nield.

Perhaps he thought that Qui-Gon still needed to gather more supplies, as he had told Obi-Wan. In that case, Obi-Wan might be planning to meet him at the starfighter. The boy had disobeyed him again, but Qui-Gon felt sure Obi-Wan would appear at the starfighter.

In any case, he couldn't waste any more time. He gathered his pack, helped Tahl to rise, and started through the tunnels to the edge of Zehava.

The smell of smoke and the sound of cries were in the air as Obi-Wan, Cerasi, and Nield climbed above ground. They crouched behind a wall for shelter. Starfighters circled overhead, strafing the park where the Young had gathered. Children ran for cover, or tried to shoot down the ships with shoulder-mounted torpedo launchers. The starfighters were able to stay out of range.

"They're wasting ammunition!" Nield cried.

"They must have flown in the starfighters from another base," Cerasi said. "Or maybe they'd hidden them somewhere we didn't know about. We can't fight them from the ground!"

Obi-Wan gripped the wall. A starfighter came in low. He saw rapid flashes from the forward gun pod. Blaster fire ripped into the grass. A young girl sprang for cover. Another boy wasn't so lucky. The fire hit him in the leg, and he fell. Before Obi-Wan could move, the boy's companion dragged him to safety. Anguish ripped through Obi-Wan. The children were helpless!

Cerasi squeezed her eyes shut, as though she couldn't bear to see any more. "We have to stop this," she said numbly.

"There's only three starfighters," Obi-Wan said tensely, scanning the sky above.

"That's enough," Nield said grimly. "We've

got to get organized. They're going to drive half of us out of the city if we don't do something!"

Nield turned to Obi-Wan. "We need your starship again, my friend. We have to fight them in the air. With your skills, we can shoot them down, just like we hit those deflection towers."

Stricken, Obi-Wan gazed at his friends. "You said you would not ask me to go against Qui-Gon's orders again."

"But everything's changed, Obi-Wan," Cerasi pleaded. "Look around you. Children are dying. We'll lose everything if we can't fight them from the air." Tears ran down Cerasi's cheeks. "Please."

Obi-Wan's ears rang with the cries of the terrified children. Even though he was safe behind the wall, he felt as though blaster fire had ripped through his body. He had been torn in two. Everything he'd known, everything he'd thought was important had been shattered. His Jedi training lay in pieces at his feet. It meant nothing compared to what was going on around him now.

He flinched as a proton torpedo exploded. Dirt sprayed into the air, raining down on their heads.

"Obi-Wan!" Nield shouted. "You must choose!"

Tears snaked down through the grime on

Cerasi's face. She didn't speak. Her shoulders shook as a child screamed in pain.

Obi-Wan realized he had already chosen. He couldn't turn his back on this suffering. He couldn't turn his back on his friends. Even if it cost him everything. He would give that, and more.

"I'll be back," Obi-Wan promised, and took off.

CHAPTER 19

Obi-Wan ran without stopping. He had to get to the ship before Qui-Gon. He did not want a confrontation. If Qui-Gon tried to stop him, what would he do? He pushed aside the thought. He would just have to get there first. Tahl would slow Qui-Gon down.

But he had underestimated the determination and speed of two Jedi Knights. As he ran down the canyon path, Obi-Wan saw Qui-Gon lifting off the last of the camouflaging branches. Tahl must already be aboard.

His steps slowed as Qui-Gon caught sight of him. Obi-Wan saw the relief on his Master's face. Qui-Gon thought he was coming to return with him to the Temple. The Jedi Knight stood by the entrance ramp, waiting.

Obi-Wan didn't give Qui-Gon a chance to speak. He could not bear to hear words of welcome.

"I'm not here to go with you," he said. "I came for the starfighter."

Qui-Gon's look of quiet welcome faded. His features froze into a mask.

"Tahl is aboard," Qui-Gon said. "I am taking her to Coruscant."

"I'll bring the ship back," Obi-Wan tried. "I need it now. If you could wait here —"

"No," Qui-Gon said angrily. "No, Padawan. I will not make your betrayal easy for you. If you try to take this step, know what a hard one it is."

Neither had moved a muscle. Yet Obi-Wan knew that Qui-Gon was just as prepared as he was to fight. The Force swirled around him, but it was a disturbed Force, neither dark nor light. He tried to tap into it and could not. It was like trying to squeeze a handful of fine sand as it streamed out through the cracks in his fingers.

He had no choice. The world around him was dying. He had to save it. He had to fight Qui-Gon.

Obi-Wan went for his lightsaber. Qui-Gon moved only a fraction of an instant later. Because of his quickness, his lightsaber activated at the same time as Obi-Wan's.

Qui-Gon's green beam shot up, glowing in the gray light. Obi-Wan felt his own lightsaber pulse in his hand. Qui-Gon kept his eyes on Obi-Wan.

Here was the moment. He had only to step forward and challenge his Master. He had only to move one muscle for it to be taken as an offensive move. Then the battle would begin.

Obi-Wan met Qui-Gon's gaze and saw the same anguish he felt. He felt something within him crack, and his resolve slowly drained away. He could not do this.

Simultaneously, they both lowered their weapons. The lightsabers deactivated with a faint buzzing sound.

For a moment, all Obi-Wan heard was the lonesome wind, howling through the canyon.

"You must choose, Obi-Wan," Qui-Gon told him quietly. "You can go with me now, or stay. Know that if you stay, you are no longer a Jedi."

No longer a Jedi. Was he prepared to take that step? Is this what he had come to?

The moment spun out, became timeless to Obi-Wan. Time meant nothing. The confrontation with the man he had pledged to study under, learn from, defend and support suddenly felt unreal. How did he get here? What was he doing?

But through his confusion he saw Cerasi's fierce glowing eyes, heard Nield's fervent words. He still smelled the smoke of battle, heard the desperate cries. He saw barricaded

streets and Elders too blind with hatred to notice that they were killing their planet, piece by
bloody piece. He saw them killing their own
children.

He could tell Qui-Gon about the battle he had
seen. He could try. But he had tried before. Qui-
Gon was right. He must make his choice.

Obi-Wan grasped the rock of his conviction
and felt his confusion drop away. Here on Melida/
Daan he had met a reality that was stronger
than anything he'd known.

"I have found something here more important than the Jedi code," Obi-Wan said slowly.
"Something not only worth fighting for, but
worth dying for."

Obi-Wan handed his lightsaber to Qui-Gon.
"You may go, Qui-Gon Jinn. But I will stay."

It was as though the words hit Qui-Gon in the
face, for he flinched. He stared down at Obi-
Wan's lightsaber in his hand, not speaking. A
great struggle seem to go on within the Jedi
Knight's powerful body.

Obi-Wan had hurt him. He longed to take the
words back. He could not. They had been said.
He had meant them.

Qui-Gon did not look at him. He did not say a
word. He turned and strode up the ramp, into
the starfighter.

Obi-Wan stood back as the engines powered up. The starfighter rose cleanly from the canyon and shot off into the upper atmosphere.

He stood watching until it was out of sight. Then Obi-Wan turned his back. He hurried down the path, back to Zehava and his new life.

Cerasi and Nield were waiting.

Discover how it
all began.

STAR WARS

JEDI APPRENTICE #6:
THE UNCERTAIN PATH

by Jude Watson

**Obi-Wan Kenobi has
left the Jedi in order to live
in a world where his youth
promises him great
power...and great danger.
Can he survive on his own?**

Coming to bookstores this January.

Visit us at www.scholastic.com

Discover how it all began.

STAR WARS

JEDI APPRENTICE